# UNDER A STERN REIGN

by

## RAYMOND WILDE

Published by **CHIMERA**
ISBN 9781780807553

# Prologue

Quite a few people are responsible for this work. It has a story.

Three years ago, I had just taken up my first appointment as a lecturer at a small university by a seaside town in Britain. I'd just turned thirty, and had been lucky in life. I wanted for little, but had just ended a relationship with my girlfriend of twelve years.

It was taking me a while to get used to being without Samantha. We had been close. Aged around eighteen we met at university, got drunk together, made love, lived together, and as years passed, we began to know each other's minds and bodies like the back of our hands.

Marriage and mortgage were becoming our main talking points. I was the nicest guy she had met, she told me, and I had not met any other girl quite like her.

But one day she began feeling her life was still unfulfilled. She was twenty-nine. It bothered her. She wanted to go her own way. She wanted to travel, to experience new things. And so that's what she did.

The bug was in her for a long time. I got postcards every few months, from Australia, Asia, and Latin America, where she either worked or backpacked, or stayed with new friends. For the last year Amsterdam has been her base. She works there for several months as a tour operator. She says she misses me but she believes she took the right decision.

Anyway, after she left I slowly settled into a reticent lifestyle, giving lectures on French Literature and History in the day. Life was lonely, spent occasionally flirting with Jeanette, a nice homely secretary in the department, and I'd generally meet up with Marianne every other evening.

Marianne was a bespectacled feminist and an enthusiastic but nervous lecturer. She was giving a course on the Spanish Cinema. I took an interest in some of her interests, and life rolled on quietly for several months until the start of the summer term.

A week in to which the students' photocopier downstairs in the French department broke. A notice was taped on telling them that they would temporarily have to do their copying in the library. All of them accepted this as law, except for one - Natalie.

Natalie was a very attractive, twenty-one-year-old blonde from Toulouse and had transferred to the university from another city-based university. She had to spend a year abroad as part of her course.

She had gone back to sunny Toulouse to recover, and with a glowing tan, she reluctantly arrived back in Britain to start the term, and complete her course requirements.

Rather than go to the library to use the other copier, Natalie discovered it was quicker and more convenient to go upstairs, find a photocopier in one of the lecturer's empty offices and to do her copying there.

As a bonus, she would not have to use her photocopying card and saved money. She chose the machine in my office and started copying away to her heart's content.

Our first encounter was on a Thursday afternoon.

The previous evening I had been gorging on Spanish wines and tortillas, watching the 1960s Luis Bunuel film *Belle de Jour*, made in France, with Marianne.

We had discussed it tipsily for quite a while. I didn't like it. I felt it was just an old, self-consciously erotic film that dabbled with sadomasochistic themes while trying to attach some deeper meaning to itself for the sake of it at the end.

Marianne disagreed. She thought it was great. She also confessed that, while she had never really experienced any lesbian or dominatrix tendencies, the pretty blonde masochist and heroine of the film was the one and only woman who had ever aroused them in her. She told me this as if uncovering one of her deepest and darkest secrets. She got a bit flirtatious, too. I told her she could confide in me, but I still didn't think the film was that good.

It was on that Thursday afternoon the next day that I came across Natalie for the first time, using the photocopier in my office.

She dazzled me. She was beautiful.

She had long blonde hair and wore tight, faded jeans over a neat bottom and slender legs. She had a pair of sunglasses perched on her head. On top, she had a hippy-style blouse and an ornate, brass-ringed belt hung around her hips.

For some reason she threw my mind back to the young blonde heroine in the film and the conversation with Marianne the previous evening. She wasn't like her, though. Natalie was more voluptuous than elegant. Though slender, she had a round, full bum and wide hips.

Her face was similar to the heroine, but lacked the serene demureness. She had a perkier nose, very full lips, angular cheekbones, and a glowing tan. She continued doing her copies while I headed for my desk, looking up at me without a smile.

I watched her for a moment or two, preparing to tell her off but suspended in a kind of dumb, aesthetic appreciation. She's French, I told myself; maybe this is a cultural thing.

She was chewing gum thoughtfully. She finished her copies, still watching me with a sort of pouting curiosity. Then without saying a word, she strolled out of the room.

It happened again the following afternoon. It was Friday, and again I sat back with my eyebrows slightly raised, simply staring at her.

Her smile, after a while, gave her away. I was a sucker for a pretty face, she had decided. It wasn't just a cultural thing; she'd discovered she could exploit me by exploiting her own looks. In French, she lazily asked me what I was doing on the weekend, as casually as if I were another student. I told her I had work to catch up on and that I needed to do lots and lots of photocopying. She shrugged, and said she'd see me next week.

The photocopier downstairs had been fixed by Monday, but on the next Thursday afternoon I was sitting at my desk, quite immersed in correcting an essay, when she turned up again.

This time her appearance didn't just leave me dumbfounded. She had dressed for the occasion, and dressed to impress. It was unbelievable. Granted it was hot outside, but nonetheless, all the other students, male and female, stuck to their semi-uniform jeans, baggy T-shirts, sweaters, overcoats and boots - all except Natalie.

She sauntered into my room, swaying her hips like a lazy pendulum, closing the door. Her sunglasses were down over her eyes.

She had snugly encased her splendid bottom in a tight black miniskirt. On top she wore a skin-tight black tank-top. Her breasts budded out as if resentful of being

3

covered over, and her nipples were clearly outlined like trapped peanuts. She also wore a thin gold chain around her neck, her throat and shoulders looking as fit and supple as a ballerina's. She was a Hollywood starlet on the way to a casting couch.

What an earth did people think when she went around the provincial streets of this academic town?

Her straw-blonde hair was tied back in a bun, and unlike the previous Friday, she wore lipstick and eye shadow. I looked at her shapely legs. She wore pumps and a gold chain around one ankle.

She looked at me from behind her tinted shades, and ignoring me, headed straight for the photocopier. I eyed her in silence for a few moments, my jaw hanging. I just could not understand what someone who looked the way she looked was doing in this dreary town, in my dreary, book-lined office.

Again I started preparing a carefully worded remonstrance. I wanted to make it as light-hearted as possible. This could all be a wind up, I thought; be charming but stay on top.

I took a few papers and stood behind her, acting as if I were in a queue for the machine. I smelled her perfume. She was a head shorter than me, and my eyes strayed over her body. She noticed. She wore no bra. I was sure she wore no panties either.

She was chewing gum again. Without looking up she asked me if I was married, or if I had a girlfriend. I shook my head. She was surprised. She didn't have a partner in this little town either, and had not met anyone she liked very much. She looked down at the copies coming out of the machine, and started to hum.

'I'm not supposed to be doing this, am I?' She smiled mischievously, looking up. 'But you don't mind...'

'What makes you say that?'

'I can tell. You like me. You want me to come here to do my copies all the time.'

I couldn't believe what I was hearing. I was silent for a moment, and then I laughed. 'I think you're very cheeky...' I started, but she giggled.

'Is that why you like to look at my bum when I turn around?' she said.

I fell silent again. She was swaying her hips and humming while watching the photocopier. She looked up. Her swaying and her accent had made my heart quicken. But her sunglasses irritated me; I couldn't see her eyes and couldn't tell what her game was. 'One of these days someone's going to put you over their knee and give you a good spanking,' I warned playfully, although deep down I meant it and dreamt of being that lucky person.

She fell silent, then giggled again. 'Spank me?' she whispered. 'Nobody *here* would do that.' She turned to the copier, humming again.

I was silent. She looked at me, then very slowly raised her sunglasses, perched them on her head, leant forward slightly, and to my astonishment, slowly hitched up her sexy miniskirt.

'Professor Wilde,' she continued huskily, 'would you want to spank this?'

The skirt seemed to roll up like a tight blind, forming a band around her narrow waist. She had shiny, painted fingernails, and massaged her pert bottom gently.

I gazed down at her in disbelief. Her bottom was gorgeous, and I was right; she wore no panties. I gulped, entranced. Her shapely buttocks were like a perfect peach, and showed the very clear outline of a bikini bottom on tanned thighs. She turned slightly, and her pussy was shaved! She was showing off her deliciously naked pussy

4

to me!

I looked up incredulously, and her face shone with triumphant impertinence. I looked down at her impeccable French rump for a few seconds again. and seeing my gaze she tautened her buttocks, stretching over the photocopier, clearly conscious of how sensual her pose. She was offering me a better look.

On her left buttock she had a small tattoo. It was a heart encircled with chains, and above it the name *Laurianne* was etched in gothic letters.

'You like the view?' she asked. 'So, what is the problem, professor?'

It was a turning point. I had to make a choice about where things stood, so I pulled my hand back very suddenly and slapped my palm fiercely across her buttocks.

She gasped softly, more out of shock than anything. I waited a second or two, then slapped again. She squealed, and then sighed a sexy coo of Gallic female pleasure.

There were footsteps and voices passing outside my door. I froze and looked over my shoulder, and she immediately pulled down her skirt. We both waited silently, watching each other.

'That is bizarre,' she whispered. 'Nobody is usually here except you at this time.'

'It's Jeanette and Professor Keating,' I said quietly. 'They're leaving.' The footsteps and chatter faded away down a flight of stairs as she straightened her top around her breasts and told me she understood why I lived alone. Solitude was preferable to being with someone you did not want to be with - like her ex-boyfriend.

I was admiring the healthy golden hew of her skin and the liveliness of her blue eyes, and then it happened. Some of her papers slipped to the floor. She dropped quickly to pick them up, and rising, inadvertently bumped my crotch with her forehead.

Her sunglasses fell off, and seeing them on the floor she dropped again, this time slowly brushing her face against my groin, marking the front of my trousers with her lustrous lipstick. I doubled slightly, totally unsure of how to react.

She rose, brushed her hand over the bulge of my erect penis, and smiled at me with the calmest complicity. We stared at each other. We knew what would happen next.

I pulled her to me, cupped her face and kissed her. She wore no bra. I fondled her breasts, peeled down her top, pulled her skirt back up, and started groping voraciously.

She unbuckled my belt, and my trousers fell to my ankles. She grasped my cock and began rubbing. I stooped and kissed her breasts like a starving man. She stopped me, took out her chewing gum, steered me towards my desk, and then I fucked her hard and hurriedly against it.

It heralded the beginning of a three month relationship that was almost entirely sexual. I poured guilt on myself for getting involved. I was also terrified of losing my job. I had visions of appearing in a newspaper and never being able to teach again.

We'd make love in my office at first. She started giving me blowjobs while footsteps and voices could be heard in the corridor outside, then after a week or so she spotted the gown and mortarboard hanging on the back of my door. Baring her buttocks she dared me to spank her, so I did. We found a cane and started using that, too.

The town was too small and nosy for us to go out anywhere together, and I think this was what began killing the relationship; Natalie wanted to be seen. Going to college each day was a kind of fashion event for her. She'd experiment with clothing, and as our relationship continued her clothes became more and more provocative. She wanted to be proud, to flaunt her affair with a young professor. She loved taking risks, and this became draining.

I needed someone to confide in so I told Marianne, but it didn't help. Marianne made me feel like a monster about it and increased my concerns by continually stressing how serious the consequences would be if I got caught. So gradually Natalie and I began to bicker as the months passed.

She wasn't a very communicative person, and what she did say would often leave me confused, curious, jealous or insecure. To surprise her once I told her about the Buñuel film, about how she vaguely resembled the heroine and about Marianne's feelings for the character. I playfully suggested all three of us go to bed together.

To my surprise she didn't object, until I pointed Marianne out to her one day and she frowned with dissatisfaction. How could I have such bad taste?

Slowly though, aspects of her life became revealed.

Her boyfriend had been handsome but brutish, so she went off men. She hated studying, she didn't want to live in wet and cold Britain any more, and she had a female friend in Toulouse who was a photographer and artist. Laurianne de Agora was her name. She was a genius, and Natalie modelled for her. She had made a fair amount of money through modelling, although she would prefer to be an actress. She also liked dancing.

The snippets of details about her friend in Toulouse made me jealous. Natalie worshipped the woman. She kept her picture, and Laurianne was about eight or nine years older than her and an attractive brunette, of a sultry Spanish appearance. Natalie had clippings of her modelling assignments, her portfolio mainly conventional lingerie. But her friend's pictures of her were nudes and erotica, with a masochist theme. She looked stunning in them. There was something between them, I felt. They were so comfortable and clearly enjoyed working together. But it was none of my business, she told me.

As the summer holidays approached I started making plans for us to travel abroad. I pictured us basking on beaches, shopping, sightseeing, dining out freely and continuing our lovemaking each night. But it was then that she dropped her bombshell.

She wanted to end the relationship. She missed her friend, and wanted to go back to France.

I took it gracefully. We still keep in touch.

She dropped out of college in France and moved in with her friend. She set her sights on acting, and appeared on calendars and in a few girlie magazines. She danced at a club and on pop videos, but couldn't get into mainstream acting at all, which was sad because she was beautiful and talented.

Her friend, meanwhile, added holistic massage to her skills, and they both now live in a rustic hillside chalet near Lausanne, Switzerland. Natalie still writes and sends the odd photo of herself, and has invited me to visit her.

Her departure from my life blew a hole through me at the time. I decided I still needed to go away, so I picked a destination out of a hat. It happened to be Lisbon, Portugal.

The city was remarkably beautiful, but the sight of so many tourists, and so many happy couples, only brought home my sense of loneliness. I decided to hire a car and go exploring.

The guidebook led me to the town of Sintra, up in the hills beside Lisbon. It was a breathtaking area, steeped in history and natural beauty. I headed off on winding roads through rich, verdant forests and rolling hills.

At one point I was running out of petrol. The area was dotted with quintas, stately homes and farmhouses that had formerly belonged to nobility. Apparently many of them had been converted into hotels and bed and breakfasts run by aristocratic descendants. I drove past a few, the advertising outside and the standardised menus off-putting. Eventually, though, I spotted one rather isolated looking quinta with no big signs by the entrance, so I gave it a try.

It turned out to be a home and not a hotel. An elderly woman lived there alone. I apologised, my Portuguese lapsing into French. She laughed, chatted with me in an odd French accent and invited me in.

She turned out to be a very sweet woman, and luckily did not automatically assume that the man at her door was a psychopath or an escaped lunatic. Instead she asked me about myself. She was cooking, and offered me dinner.

It was a rustic place with a kind of impoverished grandeur. Goats were loosely tethered in the backyard, cats spread themselves on sofas, and a dog lazily licked its private parts on the porch in the evening breeze. She offered me a drink and took a polite interest in my French teaching.

Paintings lined the hallway, and she took evident pleasure in showing them to me. The first two made me fall silent.

They were of two very pretty blondes, who looked a little like Natalie. The first had the name Genevieve de Montfort inscribed below; the other was simply called Emelie.

Next to them was a handsome man of dark appearance with piercing blue eyes. His portrait had a distinctly Byronic quality. He was called Rodolfo de Agora, and he wore some sort of uniform with decorations.

Beside him was a dark-haired female with captivating eyes and a sensual mouth. She was called Elise de Tranville.

The old lady informed me that some of them were ancestors of hers, but unfortunately records did not reveal from which of them she was descended. Archives suggested that in their lifetime a number of scandalous rumours were floating around about them.

While her husband had died and her family moved away, her origins could be traced back to both French and Portuguese nobility, she said proudly. The portraits were painted at around the time of the French Revolution, and the dark-haired gentleman had left them their family name - de Agora.

This historical theme really got the ball rolling, as I had often planned to write a novel set during the French Revolution. She wanted to help and became excited.

Two of those painted - Elise and Genevieve - kept journals during that period, she told me. They had not been published, and were still with her family.

I became curious, partly given the academic value of such journals and partly with a sense of the financial value they might represent. So I asked to see them. But they were no longer with her; her son had taken them to Geneva, where he worked as a financial consultant. He considered them too valuable to leave with her.

There were, however, some copies made. The journals were getting much the worse for wear by the turn of the century, and in 1921 her grandfather had them typed up.

Two photocopies were later made and they were with her.

Apparently, due to the fading of the family fortunes her grandfather contemplated publishing them, but censorship and decency laws and the sensitivity of their nature prevented him. So, the journals never saw the light of day.

I became increasingly curious as to what exactly would be considered worthy of censorship, given the age of the texts. The old lady didn't know, as like many other generations of her family, she was never allowed to read them. And when finally the opportunity arose her eyesight had waned, as had her interest. She had an inkling of what they might be about, though, she laughed mischievously... because of the *other* paintings.

We dined together, and after coffee I began to worry about the time. It was then that she suggested I sleep over. Her generous hospitality was so great that I felt guilty as well as odd, but I really fancied the chance of reading the copies of the journals that night, so I accepted, and as the evening came to an end I was thrilled when she finally said she would get them for me. She needed to fetch them from the basement and asked me to accompany her.

The basement was reached by a long flight of steps, and as she turned on the light she laughed and told me to take a look at the other paintings, whereupon I fell silent again. Painted over two hundred years ago, they were an assortment of nude and erotic works that would be considered broadminded even by today's standards. They involved subjects reminiscent of the females in the paintings upstairs, as well as a range of others. Their condition was poor, though.

The old lady smiled to me as I gazed at them, then handed me a bundle of yellowish, dog-eared papers tied loosely together.

I didn't sleep that night.

The journals threw me into a sort of feverishness shortly after I began reading, and it continued long into the early hours.

As I started I assumed they would more or less blend the everyday lives of people of their classes with some notable, perhaps, fresh accounts of the revolution that would be of academic interest, but instead I found two extremely intimate accounts by two very passionate women. Their experiences merged with each other's, so the same incidents were described from two perspectives.

As they were, though, they were disconnected and deeply personal. They were also in antiquated French. So it occurred to me that they could be translated and put together as one book, forming a whole, and with an omniscient narrator.

The next morning I raved excitedly about the project, and the old lady laughed at my enthusiasm. However, permission would need to be sought from her son, the holder of the original copies. She gave me his details before I left and allowed me to hold on to one of the photocopied versions.

I faxed him as soon as I got home, outlining a brief proposal, and to my surprise he not only faxed me back twenty minutes later telling me to go to hell, but also telephoned me later to make threats. Unlike other members of his family he had actually read the journals, he explained heatedly. They were scandalous and depraved, he judged, and it was for this reason that he decided they were not to be sold or reproduced in any form. For the sake of heritage they had been preserved as best as possible, but would forever remain in a family vault. I complained over his reaction and he immediately threatened me with legal action, or worse.

So I grudgingly let it all go. The photocopied journals remained on a shelf in my study and were later transferred to a box in the loft. I got on with work at the university, but it became hard, and I thought it was the latent effects of the break-up with Natalie. It was difficult settling back to a quiet life in a tiny town without our wild afternoon adventures.

I thought I might also be missing Samantha, or that I was trapped in an immature reluctance to deal with a dull life. Embarrassingly I started flirting more frequently, with Jeanette, with female students, and with a waitress.

Marianne warned me to take it easy, and then one night as we watched another arty film I drank too much and ended up making love to her.

It wasn't so bad. Without her glasses and with a little care she wasn't unattractive, and a relationship developed between us for the next year. She was a calming and caring influence. I had been neglecting things around the home, and despite her strong feminist leaning, she felt sorry for me and started helping out. I even gave her the keys Samantha had left behind.

Life went on, and then Marianne began to change. She used contact lenses instead of glasses and wore make-up. She let her hair grow long and had it styled. She'd been going to the gym and there was a distinct femininity about her clothes. It was a complete transformation, and she looked good.

So it hurt when she announced her plans. She'd decided to resign and take up a post teaching English in Barcelona. I was dumped again, it seemed.

And then I got a call from Switzerland, from Madame de Agora's son, Eduardo. It took me a while to remember who he was, and then he asked if I still had the copy of the journals. He had retired and regretted his belligerent dismissal of my approach about writing the book. Since retirement he had become an avid reader, and his literary views had changed. He apologised for having been so judgemental, and asked if I'd still be interested in carrying out the proposal I'd made, to which, somewhat surprised, I agreed.

I completed the book not long ago, and noted that something must have been happening to me while I worked. I no longer feel like the same person as when I started. It's as if I haven't been sure of whether the stupor in which the characters held me has somehow taken me over, or if I belong more in it than out of it...

I've called Samantha, and I've accepted her invitation to stay with her in Amsterdam for a while. I've also called Marianne and she's invited me over to Spain.

Lastly I got in touch with Natalie, for the first time in eight months. She says she would be delighted if I went over there too. She's told her artist friend about me, and two weeks ago she sent me another photo. She looks as stunning as ever, and wondered if I remembered the day she came in to use my photocopier.

# Chapter One

Count Guillaume de Tranville chewed on his lip and tapped his foot. His anticipation was making him restless as he leaned over the wall of one of the two turrets at the front of his home, Chateau Tranville, a small castle and former mediaeval fortress in the Loire Valley that the de Tranvilles had possessed since the inhabitants of the nearest town, Rency, could remember.

Guillaume de Tranville was waiting to see a familiar coach winding along the country road and heading for the narrow stone bridge at the castle's entrance. The count was a widower in his early fifties and had dressed more attentively than usual that day. He was a ruddily handsome man of medium height, with cropped iron-grey hair beneath his wig. He also had cloudy, grey-blue eyes that managed to hide not only the traces of grief that were still buried in him since the death of his wife some six years past, but also the knots of anxiety caused by the turn of events that had befallen France.

The radical upheavals in Paris after the storming of the Bastille in July 1789 had been too distant to disturb de Tranville in his quiet, provincial abode, and he had not felt it necessary to leave the country along with many of his friends that year.

But the bloody purges that swept through the land from the summer of 1793 now wracked him with worry. He would often spend his nights pacing nervously up and down in his bedchamber, unable to find sleep.

The Reign of Terror, and the betrayals, arrests and executions of noblemen suspected of being counter-revolutionaries presented him with far greater danger than ever before. So many of his well-to-do friends and acquaintances in Paris and the provinces had been rounded up like cattle and butchered simply because of their aristocratic blood and a handful of wild allegations by resentful commoners calling themselves officials.

And he knew the same fate could befall him. Only seven months earlier his harmless, dear old friend, the Marquis de Montvert, had been executed along with all but one member of his family.

De Tranville remained reluctant to flee France, though, as apparent as the dangers of the revolution now were. His fears had become too well counterbalanced by both the love he felt for his ancestral home and his adulterous relationship with a local woman who would not agree to leave with him, should he ever ask her to.

She was a buxom, discreetly licentious brunette, and the wife of the local town mayor. She had indulged in numerous affairs during her fourteen-year marriage and the count prized her as a seasoned and urbane lover. They had begun their afternoon liaisons the previous year, and as the relationship grew so his sense of personal safety waned.

But at nights the fears flooded back and his dreams became interspersed with visions of his old friends being hounded by predatory bureaucrats, chained in stinking dungeons and decapitated before jubilant, bloodthirsty mobs.

But the turbulent times were far from the count's mind on that warm April afternoon in the year of 1794, as he eagerly awaited his mistress. Her arrival was seldom punctual and there was still no sight of her. But he could see his dark-haired stepdaughter Elise, walking with their new lodger Genevieve. The sweet young blonde was the daughter of his close friend, de Montvert, guillotined in Lyons seven months earlier.

Watching Elise walking with Genevieve on the other side of the bridge sent a shiver through the count; the previous day he was gazing at the portrait of his wife in the library. When Elise's mother had been taken from the world suddenly by pneumonia six winters ago, she left the count too devastated to pay much attention to her sulky teenage daughter. But the girl had truly blossomed. She was now even more darkly beautiful than the sultry beauty he married eight years before.

It was strange how life could rob him of his wife and now replace her with these two beauties. Together they seemed like night and day, and either of them could stir the passions of even the most lackadaisical of men. They were his, though neither belonged to him in blood, and neither belonged to him in bed.

For a fleeting moment he imagined himself being the lover of both young women. He studied them and pictured himself showering kisses on the napes of each of their graceful necks, caressing Genevieve's fair, svelte and silky body, nibbling the inside of Elise's warm limbs.

He imagined how he might one day find Genevieve doing something wrong, and chastise her in the library, sweeping his palm down vigorously on those virgin buttocks, as he had once done with Elise, not so long ago. Then he tried to chase the thoughts away as quickly as he always did when they occurred.

The last time he had punished Elise was a sensitive matter for him. It was two years ago and she had just turned twenty at the time. He had hired a new kitchen maid, a delightful slip of a girl, with long fair hair and doll's eyes. Genevieve vaguely reminded him of her, and he had only just started to enjoy her young body himself after instructing her to bring him his breakfast of warm chocolate and cakes each morning. He asked her to sit with him awhile on the first morning, and she did so with an enchanting smile. His loins stirred as he watched her coy face and glimpsed the upper slopes of her creamy breasts above her corset, and seeing his manhood rise beneath his nightshirt she had no qualms about taking it in her hand, as if examining some unusual object.

Despite her virginal looks the maid seemed to be acquainted with such practices. She rubbed it pleasingly and took it in her mouth, and the count was delighted in what seemed to be the start of a pleasant adventure for each morning.

But soon after he discovered the perverse relationship that had developed between the girl and Elise. The little nymph would have been such a delight, but how had she become entangled in those strange incidents with Elise?

What wicked spirits had possessed his stepdaughter at that time, and why would she be applying such cruel and intimate treatment to not only another young wench, but to the beauty he had handpicked strictly with his own pleasures in mind?

He'd had to dismiss the comely maid, with much regret and despite her sobbing tale of innocence. He recalled how lovely he had found her and her caressing lips on that first morning... and how voluptuous he found Elise's naked body as he thrashed her in his library.

The punishment had seemed to do the trick, for in the two years since he had encountered no further evidence of Elise's lusts and inclinations towards other maids.

11

It was also strange how mother and daughter could be so alike, he reflected. The hot-blooded woman with long blue-black hair and dark nature seemed to have been reborn in his stepdaughter, Elise. It was not just her looks. The girl carried herself with the same natural poise and confidence in her own desirability. And it was uncanny how, along with her beauty, she had the same way of instinctively instilling fear into servants and peasants alike. It was more than just the firmness of her voice or the coldness of her tone. There was something in the eyes. The same flickering flames when anger gripped her or when she was up to mischief.

How could someone as wilful as Elise now become so close to a girl as gentle as Genevieve de Montvert? As personalities went the golden-haired guest seemed to have little in common with Elise... except youthful beauty, of course.

The count's keen eye noted the shapeliness of Genevieve's slighter contours each time they met, and though they were not as pronounced as those of Elise, they belied the innocence of her soft eyes and announced to the world that the fruit of her womanhood was full and ready.

Unable to resist the distraction, the count again began to imagine being the lover of the girls. He imagined them naked, which was not hard to do with Elise, for he had seen her so and the delicious vision remained embedded.

From afar he studied Genevieve intently, savouring her beauty, but his musings were caught short, for a coach was moving along the road leading to Chateau Tranville. It was the wife of the local town mayor arriving at last, so he hastily chased his improper thoughts of the girls away.

Genevieve did not notice the approach of Madame Margaret Coubette's coach as she strolled with Elise. Her thoughts were too preoccupied with her companion. Her shock over the arrest of her family had overwhelmed her, but now, seven months on, she was becoming more and more absorbed by the world of de Tranville's chateau and his stepdaughter.

Seven months before a faithful elderly maid, Madeleine, managed to hide her when a revolutionary committee led a mob to her home. They took away her parents and her elder brother, Gustav. Madeleine hid her in a broom cupboard while they ransacked the de Montvert estate, and it was the last she saw of her family. The terrible news of their execution was broken to her one week after Madeleine took her by coach to Count de Tranville.

And while mourning their loss over the following days, a further loss was added. Madeleine died too, the strain of the times proving too much for her aged heart.

It took Genevieve quite some time to adjust to her new life, the count seeming distant while Elise was new to her in all ways. She was deeply shy of her at first. The thoughtful young lady was singularly attractive, but there was something so daunting in the boldness of her tone and manner.

As the months passed, though, so too did her shyness. They began to talk more freely and Genevieve became enchanted by the courteous and generous nature of her dark-haired companion, as well as the frequent compliments she paid to her own fair beauty.

It was thus, that by that afternoon in April, the two girls had found themselves enjoyably locked in conversations on a subject that was now at the top of Genevieve's interests - love. She had so many questions to ask and was intrigued by Elise's curious views.

'But why do you distrust men so?' she laughed softly as they walked together.

'Men are simply cruel boys that temporarily pretend to be poets,' Elise replied curtly. 'When they like a woman they capture her heart with beautiful ideas and words,' she explained, staring mirthfully into Genevieve's clear eyes. 'But just like spoilt boys they need to be entertained or else they get bored and roam away in search of other amusements. As boys become men they soon learn that their greatest pleasures derive from what is done to their bodies... by us, by themselves and by other men too, sometimes.' Elise whispered with mock indignation. 'At least, that is what I have seen, and learned.'

'But that is love of the senses, not true love,' Genevieve said.

'There is no distinction,' Elise continued in a hushed tone, taking Genevieve's arm. 'Love is nothing more than the satisfying of the most primitive pleasures with the person one desires at the time. It is a transient thing, as you will see for yourself soon,' she added abruptly, and turned Genevieve's waist firmly to make her face the path leading back to the castle.

Genevieve gazed at Elise bemusedly for a moment, but remained silent. Feeling a sudden quickening of her heart she remembered that, as Elise left her room the night before, she had used the same words.

Talk of love between Genevieve and Elise had grown more intense after the visit of the son of one of Count de Tranville's friends, a young Portuguese gentleman called Rodolfo, two months before. While the two girls dined with de Tranville and Rodolfo, Genevieve found herself frequently blushing as she gazed at the handsome foreigner, even though he addressed himself mainly to the count.

Through dinner she timidly stole glances at him, his healthy bronzed skin and the shiny blackness of his hair. And when Rodolfo addressed her occasionally, his wintry-blue eyes made her feel as if her insides were on fire. Elise had looked at her continually during the evening with a whimsical smile, but the glances she exchanged with him were decidedly chilly.

News that Rodolfo would be visiting again had prompted Genevieve to speak to Elise the previous evening, not just of love in general, but of the feelings for the young man she'd experienced during that dinner. The two girls chatted each night in Genevieve's room, usually after they'd bathed, and took turns in brushing each other's hair.

Genevieve had been sitting on a leather trestle by the warm wood fire in her room, freshly bathed, enjoying the feel of her nakedness beneath her cool light shift and the strokes of Elise's brush through her silky hair. It was then that she confessed her feelings towards Rodolfo during the dinner. 'I have never felt so nervous.' she reflected. 'My hands were actually trembling. I wonder if that's what love is.'

'Rodolfo is a man who takes his pleasure as and when he pleases, he is unlikely to be content with just one woman,' Elise snapped, and seeing the sting of her words in Genevieve's eyes, she laughed. 'He delights in breaking the hearts of sweet little things that know nothing of love, like you.

'Let us see... if I were you and you were Rodolfo, how would you kiss me, for example?' She was smiling broadly, revealing neat white teeth.

'Kiss you?' Genevieve started in puzzlement.

'Yes. Have you ever kissed a man?' Elise raised Genevieve gently to her feet. She stood about half a head taller and her elegant hands gently brushed Genevieve's blonde hair behind her neck and over her shoulders.

Feeling artful fingers squeezing into her soft flesh, Genevieve giggled at the game. 'You are so dashing, Rodolfo,' she found herself saying playfully, and to her own surprise she allowed her hands to gently stroke Elise's hair in return. She tried to imagine Rodolfo standing before her.

'Kiss me as you would kiss Rodolfo,' Elise commanded in a determined whisper, and Genevieve closed her eyes and moved her lips gingerly to hers, finding them as soft as petals but as warm as fire.

'That is how you would kiss a child or a friend good day,' Elise scolded mockingly, in a hushed voice, then tugged Genevieve's limp body sharply and tightly to her, her hands like pincers as they clamped on her shoulders, and Genevieve felt her friend's succulent lips pressed to hers. Elise's tongue probed into Genevieve's mouth, and as she held the blonde girl her firm breasts and stiff nipples pressed tightly against her. Genevieve felt her own nipples harden and tingle at the touch, and her heartbeat quickened.

'That is how he would probably kiss you, my silly darling,' Elise whispered as she pulled away. Intense warmth had radiated between them, leaving Genevieve glowing, heat and moisture gathering between her thighs.

'You do not love Rodolfo and he does not love you,' Elise whispered, her face so close that Genevieve could feel the warmth of her breath. 'You just think you do.'

Releasing her grip, Elise traced a circle on the side of one of Genevieve's thighs and then, with a cruel grin, she pinched her bottom sharply, making the blonde squeal and push Elise away.

'There is much you must learn in life, my sweetheart,' Elise laughed softly, withdrawing and slightly narrowing her eyes. 'But at least you have learned what a proper kiss feels like, and tomorrow you must see something very, very interesting. Something that should put an end to your silly thoughts of dashing Rodolfo.' Warmth had returned to her eyes, and she pulled Genevieve to her again, kissed her once more, bade her goodnight and left the room.

Genevieve turned and threw herself on her bed, still feeling the pinch on her bottom as if something had bitten her, but only to intensify the rhythm that had started pulsing between her thighs.

When Elise had listened to Genevieve confessing her feelings for the handsome man who dined with the count two months earlier, it was not simply cruelty that inspired her to describe Rodolfo de Agora as a man who could not be content with just one woman. During the dinner she observed with detached amusement as Genevieve's cheeks turned crimson each time Rodolfo addressed her. Together they would certainly make an attractive couple, she reflected. Sitting opposite the young man, Genevieve looked more delightful than ever. With her long blonde locks, the girl's blushing face radiated a summery beauty, while the flickering candles on the table brought out the fineness of her cheekbones and the sparkle in her blue eyes. How could a dashing young stag like Rodolfo not lose his heart to such a sweet young doe as Genevieve?

Something in his manner, however, told her that he did not quite fit the princely role. From the frequency and nature of his glances, it seemed clear that he was charmed by Genevieve's beauty, but there was also too much confidence and quiet thoughtfulness in his look. Rodolfo's eyes were not those of someone smitten, but those of someone who observes and compares, rather like her own. They were predatory eyes that roved too much. He was a false prince, she concluded.

His eyes would flicker every few minutes over both of them, resting at times on Genevieve and at times on her. He was assessing them. She could feel it when he looked at her, his eyes pausing at her face, flickering over her lips and straying down to her cleavage and the swell of her breasts above her bodice.

She would meet his eye. He was drawn to her, it was clear. When their eyes met he would smile and his eyes would move on, usually back to Genevieve. She was attracted to him. She knew it. But his eyes were more for her friend. They hovered over her just that little bit more.

That night Elise passed Genevieve's bedchamber, but instead of entering as usual she continued to the guest's bedchamber. Curiosity, among other urges, was pulling without any indication of where it would lead her. She wanted to see the man's avaricious eyes once again, and have them devouring her as they had during dinner.

Wearing nothing but her shift and with her black hair loose around her shoulders, she trod softly along the dark landing to Rodolfo's door, where she paused and listened. There was silence, except for an occasional faint rustling sound. A dim light escaped beneath the door, and she entered without knocking.

The room was dimly lit by a candle next to the guest's four-poster bed, and by the embers of a fire. She saw him on the bed, lying in flickering shadow, and let out a soft gasp.

He lay naked, his muscular limbs stretched out languidly. His eyes met hers, and in one hand he was holding his cock. It was disproportionately large, stretching lazily out of a bush of black curls. He smiled at her, stroking his half erect member.

Elise gazed at it for long moments. She had only seen two cocks in her life, and neither remotely compared with the one before her. It seemed double the size of either and would have seemed more appropriate if attached to a horse.

'At last,' he said quietly. 'Come in and close the door.'

Elise did as she was bidden, as if in a trance. She did not know what had drawn her to the room, or what to expect.

'Come closer. I've been waiting for you.' He raised himself onto his elbows, releasing his cock and letting it flop heavily against his thigh. Elise was now standing within arm's length of the bed, his eyes still fixed on hers, which were still fixed on his penis.

'And what about your lovely friend?' he continued. 'I was hoping the both of you would come along.'

'It's huge... why is it like that?' Elise murmured, spellbound.

'It's what you girls did to me. I haven't been able to get either of you out of my mind since dinner.'

Then suddenly, seeing life pulsing in Rodolfo's huge limb, Elise felt an urge to step back. It seemed to be rearing towards her, beckoning her. But as she wavered he stretched out lithely and grabbed her wrist, then rose from the bed and stood facing her.

'If you do anything to me I'll cry out,' she blurted, panicking suddenly. 'I'll scream for help.'

'Some might find it a little strange to find you here,' he pointed out, unconcerned by her weak threat. 'I knew you would come, however.' His hands rose to her face, which he cupped and stroked. 'You have such lovely lips. Now get down on your knees,' he commanded, his hands on her shoulders, firmly pressing downwards. She realised what he had in mind; he wanted her to do what the count's mistress did and she had secretly watched so often. She tried to shake off his grasp, but he strengthened his hold and pressed harder. 'On your knees.'

Again she found herself doing as ordered, as if in a trance. His stern command excited her. She knelt, alarmed by the stiff limb that nudged her chin as she sank down, thinking of what she had seen the count's mistress doing during her afternoon visits. It was her turn now. She was going to suck a man, just as Madame Coubette sucked her stepfather.

Rodolfo moved his hand under her chin, and squeezing her cheeks, he eased the head of his monstrous cock between her moist, slightly parted lips. Nervously she felt his helmet filling her, forcing her jaws to widen, pushing against the roof and back of her mouth. Its veined underside rubbed over her tongue, warm and throbbing. She tightened her lips, and as she had seen Madame Coubette doing, gently bobbed her head backwards and forwards.

'That's it,' Rodolfo sniggered dryly. 'That's very nice... very nice indeed. Have you done this often?'

Elise tried to shake her head as she continued to bob back and forth rhythmically, letting it plough in and out of her mouth, her lips clamped tightly to it. Her trepidation faded, and gradually she felt strangely powerful; the huge male thing, stretching her lips apart, was somehow hers. It was hers to control. She let it plop out of her mouth, and gazing at it, probed her tongue to its tip. She teased it with a lingering lick and smiled up at Rodolfo, who gasped as his hot seed suddenly erupted, covering Elise's chin in sticky cream as she pulled her head back, shocked by the potency of his ejaculation.

'What a delightful, naughty girl you are, Elise,' he groaned, letting out a deep sigh. Then he helped her to her feet. 'I very much hope to have the pleasure again some time.'

Elise elegantly dabbed her sleeve over her mouth, looked up into his dark eyes, and then down at his member. His limb had lost its power and now looked pacified. She had tamed and broken it like a wild horse.

'Tell me, is Genevieve quite as delightful a cock sucker as you?' he asked arrogantly, casually cupping her breasts through her shift.

'I don't know,' Elise replied coolly. 'Perhaps you'll find out one day.'

'I certainly hope so. You know, as I watched her at dinner, I felt I could almost fall for that girl.'

'And did you feel yourself almost fall for me, too?'

'In a way.' Rodolfo looked at her pensively. 'In a way, I suppose I might have done.'

Elise looked into his infuriatingly conceited expression, and something frightened her and made her heart stir.

She hastily left the room.

# Chapter Two

After her impromptu encounter with Rodolfo, the taste of the man's cock remained on her mind for a long time more than it had been in her mouth. For many days she tingled with quiet satisfaction and pride.

The affair between Count de Tranville and Madame Coubette had not been as discreet as the count supposed. Their liaisons, passionate and ritualistic, were only thinly concealed at the castle. They had long become the covert study of his manipulative stepdaughter.

She studied them from a regular vantage point - the landing that overlooked the castle's large hall and drawing room, the count's impulsiveness often leading him to enjoy his mistress there, only moments after her arrival.

Elise had been drawn by his groans mingling with Madame Coubette's cooing. She would crouch at the banisters of the landing each time Madame Coubette visited, keen to see the sight of the two lovers.

'Love is nothing more than the satisfying of the most primitive pleasures with the person one desires at the time,' she had said to Genevieve as she walked with the pretty girl on the castle lawns. 'It is a transient thing.' With the words she echoed the promise she made the previous night when she had played Rodolfo in her improvised game. Now, as she had promised, she was to take her to see something interesting, something that would open her eyes to the darker side of love.

All kinds of designs had been awakening in Elise. There was something so tender about Genevieve that excited but irked her. Desire and wilfulness filled her as she looked at her fair companion. Elise subdued her excitement as she slipped her arm around Genevieve's trim waist and led her towards the chateau. Casually she allowed her hand to rest around Genevieve's ribs, her fingers settling on the soft swell that formed the lower cup of one of the girl's breasts. She monitored the warmth of the girl's body and the detectably quickened pace of her heart, and smiled to herself. The cute doe was stirring with each subtle trick of the huntress. It was strange how all seemed to slip so easily into plan.

In Genevieve's virginal eyes Elise could see the girl's soul yearning secretly for someone strong to take her in hand. She wanted to be used by someone and as someone else pleased. She wanted to be bestowed with pleasures that she had never experienced yet quietly cried out for... to none but Elise.

Inside the chateau the girls found the count standing before the fireplace. He greeted them briskly. Madame Coubette had just arrived and burst into a smile as they entered.

'Elise, as beautiful as ever and growing more like her mother every day!' she chimed. Kissing Elise's cheek, the handsome woman beamed at her and then turned to Genevieve. 'And what a delightful young friend you have.'

'Genevieve is the daughter of the late Marquis de Montvert,' the count explained. 'I don't think you have been introduced yet. The de Montverts, old friends of mine, have fallen victim to these mad times. Genevieve is now my charge.'

'My poor orphaned angel,' sighed Coubette, her elegant face at once assuming an expression of deep pity. Her silk-gloved hand rose and lightly settled on Genevieve's cheek. She studied the girl's eyes, her fingers drifting against her cheekbone and cupping her chin.

'De Montvert and I had been the closest of friends.' The count frowned. 'Nobody is safe these days.'

'Oh, what a tragedy... and that such a beautiful young thing should be visited by such great sorrow.' Coubette's hand was still on Genevieve's cheek, and the girl looked up at the tall woman. An elaborate wig covered her hair, sparkling here and there with small gemstones, but what struck Genevieve most was the size of the woman's breasts and hips. She was so trim of waist, yet so large of bosom and rump.

'I do hope you're taking good care of your friend,' Madame Coubette said, turning to Elise.

'Why, naturally.' Briskly Elise took hold of Genevieve's arm, and Madame Coubette's lively eyes flickered over them thoughtfully.

'Perhaps, it might be opportune to let you young ladies know of a decision I have been weighing up for some time,' the count interrupted. 'The situation in France, as you may know, is becoming too dangerous. Over the last few months I have been in contact with friends outside, in England and in Portugal. In fact, my close Portuguese friend, the Conde de Agora, recently sent his son to visit us to discuss the safest itinerary and timing of a journey to that land. Rodolfo, he came to dinner, as you girls know.'

'Yes, of course,' Elise replied, and Genevieve blushed at the mention of his name.

'I am now of the opinion that leaving France will be inevitable for us. I have in mind the end of this month as the date of our departure. As it happens, Rodolfo, at his father's request, has kindly agreed to help us on our trip serving as both guide and escort.'

Madame Coubette's eyes turned cold.

'I would also like to let you know of my decision to invite you, Madame Coubette, along with us. I know it might seem like a strange proposal with little notice, but in the period of our friendship I have learned to trust you as a dear companion. It is not easy for a man to raise two young ladies. Your wisdom and assistance would be invaluable. It would be a temporary arrangement, and?'

'And my husband?' Madame Coubette interrupted.

'Naturally, you would be providing me with a service,' the count replied. 'A valuable service, and I would be willing to make it well worth its while for both you and your husband.'

Madame Coubette gazed at him in angry silence.

'It is something I would like you to consider,' the count added. 'It is no longer safe for the girls or me to remain in the country and I'd like very much for you to come with us.' He sensed Madame Coubette's hostility and turned to the girls. 'I believe you were going to your rooms?' he said.

Obediently Elise and Genevieve nodded, took leave of Madame Coubette, and headed upstairs.

The count and Madame Coubette remained silent as the girls left.

'So, you've decided it's time to leave,' Madame Coubette said when the girls were out of earshot, her eyes glinting with contempt.

18

'I have little choice. But I want you to come with us.'

'As you know I am far from being an aristocrat, or any kind of lady for that matter, and I am in absolutely no kind of peril. I have a hardworking husband, plenty of friends, plenty of leisure time... a very good life. Why on earth should I want to throw all that up to go away with you? Would you marry me? Would you make me Countess de Tranville?'

'You know that's not possible, and you know you don't feel anything for that miserable old cockroach that calls himself your husband. The whole thing can be arranged, I'm sure.'

'And I'll just follow you to wherever your cowardice leads?' Madame Coubette mocked. 'Abandon my home, country, husband and position, for you? Or just until you feel it's time to find another, younger pussy to play with, perhaps?'

As the two girls turned the corner at the top of the stairs Genevieve followed Elise's hushed instructions. She fell softly to her hands and knees, as did her companion.

Elise placed her arm around Genevieve's shoulder, signalled to her to be silent with a slender finger touched to her lips, and together they peered through the banisters, looking down through the open door of the drawing room at the developing row between the count and his voluptuous guest.

'Don't start this again,' the count growled wearily.

'Tell me, sir, is my pussy the only one that pleases you?' the woman goaded. 'But what might the pussy be like in Portugal?'

The count guffawed. 'Must you always be driven by your jealousies?'

She smiled at him and moved a gloved hand to the front of his breeches. Deftly, and without taking her eyes from his, she located his member. 'And look at this. I only have to mention the pussy in that country and the horse is ready to bolt from its stable!' In a deft move she unfastened his breeches, glanced at him, and then lowered to her knees before him. His breeches slid down to his ankles and exposed pale legs. His erect penis curved upward, pointing directly at Madame Coubette's face. She took it between both palms and stretched back the skin so that the purplish head rose and inflated a few centimetres before her lips. 'My dear sir,' she purred, before engulfing it in her mouth.

Genevieve's heart began beating quicker. The count's manhood, exposed thus, bewildered her. It seemed fearsome, even from a distance. Its shadowy veins glistened wetly as it emerged and disappeared inside the woman's avaricious maw. Genevieve glanced uncertainly at Elise, and found her friend smiling back at her.

'An essential skill for lovers,' Elise whispered, and placed her hand on Genevieve's thigh.

Allowing the count's wet cock to slide from her mouth, Madame Coubette smiled up at him, slightly out of breath. 'Come to think of it, why would you go to Portugal for your new pussy, when you have two gorgeous young pussies here with which to indulge yourself? Neither is blood of yours, though you act as though they are. Surely you've considered seducing them both? Surely you'd like to fuck them? What red-blooded male wouldn't?'

'Be quiet,' the count growled. 'Watch what you say.'

'And that Elise,' the woman went on, provoking him. 'Why, I don't think you'd find as lusty a bitch in all the brothels in France. Don't you notice the way she looks at you? I know the fantasies of young females, and I'd swear she'd give anything to be kneeling where I am now, sucking your aristocratic cock instead of me. Wouldn't you like that? Wouldn't you like it to be Elise kneeling here right now, paying homage to your cock with those sweet young lips?'

Genevieve was sure she heard the faintest of sighs coming from her companion. She glanced at her quickly, but there was no time to look for long because of the shock of what suddenly happened downstairs. An abrupt thwack resounded and was immediately followed by a yelp of indignation. It was, evidently, the count's response to Madame Coubette's provocation, and Genevieve looked back to the quarrelsome pair below.

The woman was prostrate on her front before the count, her wig several feet away, her hair, a tangled auburn mop, covered her face. Wounded more in pride than in pain, she slowly arched her spine to raise herself, and her large bottom lifted voluptuously as she turned her face to his.

He stood frowning over her, unconcerned by the blow that had knocked her flat; he knew she wasn't hurt, for the brunt of the impact had fallen on the wig. His hands were on his hips and his cock, semi-erect and now drooping, pointed down at her.

'If you talk to me like a whore from the streets, I'll treat you as such,' he said. 'I've told you that before, and I've also told you not to talk of Elise in that way.'

Through the tangles of hair Madame Coubette's eyes burned. Their glow amidst her reddened cheeks made her whole face come alive. She was a seething beast, enraged at being so crudely brought to heel. She turned away from him and crawled towards her wig, her buttocks undulating beneath her dress. Reaching the hairpiece she turned back to him with a sneer. 'I'll talk as I please,' she hissed. 'And I *am* a whore from the streets, but I can tell you, Elise is a bigger whore than me.'

De Tranville leapt at the crouching woman, snatched at the dress and fiercely tore it apart. Then with the same vicious frenzy he ripped away the petticoat beneath, leaving bare the white cheeks of her bottom. At the sight he thrust her to the floor, lashing at her nakedness with his palm. Cutting through the air fierce slaps resounded on her bared flesh, and were echoed by sighs and whimpers from her.

Genevieve felt herself swoon. De Tranville's rage seemed to fill the room below, yet it seemed somehow dank with passion. Blotches of red surfaced angrily on Madame Coubette's pallid bottom cheeks, but soon her protests melted. The blows were softening. She laid flat on her front, humiliated, her lower half stripped, her flushed cheek to the carpet. De Tranville rested on his haunches, breathing heavily.

Genevieve pushed her head forward with curiosity, her cheeks pressed to the ornately twisting columns of wood that made up the balustrade. The woman was now saying something.

'Fuck me... fuck me now,' she mumbled. 'Fuck me.'

De Tranville gazed at her coldly. She lifted herself back onto her knees and elbows, offering him her bottom, and he watched her parting the cleft between her legs for him.

'Fuck me,' she pleaded, and the count roughly clasped the tangle of hair at the back of her head and drove into her. She gasped, and keeping her hair gripped in one fist de Tranville began rutting in and out of her ferociously.

Genevieve turned to Elise, again aware of her friend. She could feel her rustling, trembling. She was busy doing something, it seemed, and Genevieve let out a faint gasp of shock. Elise was not just being a spectator. She was squatting on her calves, her bare knees spread wide, the folds of her skirt and cotton slip pulled up around her waist. She wore no knickers, and one hand was lost in the shiny black triangle of curls between her legs, her fingers rubbing in a quiet frenzy. Genevieve watched, her mouth open, as Elise's fingers traced up and down the ruby lips between her thighs.

Genevieve gulped and tore her eyes back to the scene below. The shameful noises there seemed to be subsiding. With a final groan the count threw himself heavily over Madame Coubette, bringing them both down to the carpet. Madame Coubette murmured words that Genevieve was unable to discern, and as she tried she felt Elise's hand tug on her arm.

'Time to go,' the sultry girl whispered, her cheeks decidedly flushed.

Genevieve tiptoed along the landing and noticed Elise was breathing heavily, her eyes gleaming darkly with playfulness.

'You look thoroughly startled,' Elise said quietly, closing the bedroom door behind them. 'I hope that little surprise didn't prove too much. And your dress, why, you're all crumpled.'

Genevieve's heart was still thumping as Elise stepped behind her and stooped to pad away the wrinkles around the bottom of her dress. The soft beats of the girl's hand on her thighs and calves seemed strangely soothing.

How despicably and roughly the count had treated his guest, she reflected. And yet, the ruder the treatment the more satisfied Madame Coubette had seemed to become. The shameful encounter still held her in a trance, her mouth dry, her hands clammy, her loins throbbing again just like the night when Elise had kissed her, pretending to be Rodolfo. She shyly pressed her thighs together, Elise still padding her skirts.

'So, what do you think?' Elise whispered, straightening up. She bore the same smile she had that previous night, a pearly smile of mischief carved on sultry beauty.

'It was certainly a shock,' Genevieve admitted. 'A huge shock.'

Elise giggled softly. 'And how did you feel? Did you enjoy the spectacle? Wouldn't you like Rodolfo to do that to you?' Genevieve shrugged awkwardly, and Elise stepped behind her and with a jolt, caught her hips, making her gasp with surprise. 'Wouldn't you like Rodolfo to take you like that? Like a stallion enjoying his mare?' Mockingly she ground her pelvis against Genevieve's buttocks, and the girl giggled nervously. They were standing close to the four-poster bed, and with another thrust Genevieve lost her balance and with Elise's hands still on her hips, tumbled onto the bed.

'I don't know,' she muttered from under Elise, who rose and strolled towards the room's latticed windows. She gazed out for a moment, then casually loosened the cord that held back one of the heavy curtains, and the room became shadowy as it fell across the window.

'Is it true that the count is going to take us to Portugal, and that Rodolfo is going with us?' Genevieve asked.

'It's the first I've heard of it,' Elise said dryly, then drew the other curtain, the room now lit by only one beam of sunlight through the gap between them. She sauntered pensively back to the bed, the cords of the curtains dangling in her hands. Genevieve watched her blankly.

'He seemed so rough with her... is it always like that?' she asked timidly.

'No, not always.' Elise laid the cords on the bed and unbuttoned the bodice of her dress.

'The... um... the count seemed enchanted when she kissed, um, his...' Genevieve went on distractedly.

'Of course; it's one of the most pleasing things a man can experience.' Elise pulled open her bodice and stood bare-breasted in front of the spellbound girl, then let the dress drop to the floor. She stood there quietly, looking deeply into Genevieve's eyes, and let her hands cup her breasts and run over her nipples. They were large and pointed stiffly. 'I become so hot when I watch them together.' She raised her hands from her breasts to push her raven hair off her shoulders. Her full breasts swayed provocatively with her movements. 'It's as if my body catches fire.' She unfastened the buttons at the waist of her white cotton slip, her eyes on Genevieve's, then let it drift to the floor and stood naked for the first time in front of her lovely friend.

The sight held the supine girl speechless as she shyly looked at her friend's toned body, utterly shocked that she wore nothing appropriate beneath her dress, and by the admission that she'd spied on the count and his mistress before.

Elise turned and moved gracefully to the wardrobe. Her bottom formed a perfect oval and seemed to glow with sensual warmth. She met Genevieve's eyes as she moved back to the bed with a bundle of clothes in her arms.

'This dress is a little small for me now,' she said. 'I chose it two years ago but I've never worn it. Try it on. It's time you considered your clothing more... especially if you're to meet Rodolfo again. Come on, get undressed.'

Somewhat bewildered by the turn of events, and as though in a dream, Genevieve began unbuttoning her blouse. She slowly opened it and shivered, the outline of her nipples pressing into her white cotton camisole.

Elise got on the bed and straddled Genevieve's waist, her firm breasts hovering a few inches from her face. 'Come on,' Elise whispered urgently, and unbuttoned Genevieve's skirt and petticoat, her fingers cool against Genevieve's bare hip.

'Why is it such a pleasing thing?' she asked.

'Lift your bottom,' Elise commanded, and as Genevieve obeyed she pulled down her skirt, petticoat and knickers in one go, leaving her naked from the waist down.

'Why is it so pleasing for a man?' she asked again, modestly crossing her arms over her breasts.

'It's a secret pleasure,' Elise told her cryptically. 'Pleasures that can only be experienced and not explained.'

Elise moved and sat at the foot of the bed, resting back against one of the ornate posts. Genevieve continued to gaze in nervous awe at the naked beauty of her friend.

'As a matter of fact, I forgot to tell you,' Elise went on conspiratorially. 'Rodolfo and I shared the very same pleasure only recently. The night he was here.'

Genevieve's cheeks turned crimson. She instantly forgot about how cool she felt and how strange it was to be virtually naked before her friend. Casually, Elise stroked the dark curls of her own pubis. 'I wouldn't worry your pretty little head about it too much, though,' she said. 'As I kissed him he professed how taken he was with you. Your problem, though, will be that you will never be able to keep him,' Elise mocked with unnecessary cruelty. 'There are too many temptations for him. Too many who know how to please him better. There is so much you must learn, poor naïve Genevieve.'

'What must I learn?' the girl asked, propping herself on her elbows, acutely aware of her nakedness, and her friend's, and the strangeness of it. She swallowed nervously;

there was something that felt good about it. She did not want to reach for her clothes. There was something so hungry in Elise's dark eyes, and it made her feel vulnerable.

She glanced furtively at Elise's idly moving hand, at the index finger tracing a circle at the top of the pink lips. Her other hand moved slowly over her ribcage, cupping her left breast, allowing the nipple to peep between massaging fingers. Then opening her eyes and observing Genevieve's confused expression, Elise laughed quietly.

'Lie back,' she ordered, and Genevieve instinctively fell back against the pillows, and as she did she felt Elise's warm body rising over her again. 'Pretend I'm Rodolfo,' she whispered, and then she leant down to kiss the befuddled girl.

Genevieve closed her eyes, the soft lips of her friend drifting over her face and throat. Her body pulsed with forbidden excitement, her heart ready to burst.

Elise cupped Genevieve's firm breasts, shuffled down a little, and took a nipple between her lips. Genevieve shivered, and instinctively pressed a hand to the back of Elise's head. Elise kissed the other budding breast, furtively watching her companion tremble under her lascivious attention from beneath lowered lashes. Then she moved again and her tongue passed over her flat tummy until it reached the soft nest of blonde curls she sought.

With her eyes tightly closed, Genevieve held her breath and felt her heart ready to explode. Her pussy was wet, she knew. Elise paused, and then licked lightly a few times, drawing a sob from her friend. Elise paused again, watching her responses, and then locating Genevieve's clitoris with her fingertips, she targeted it with her tongue. Another soft whimper and spasm drifted from Genevieve's breathless frame.

Elise raised her face, her chin and lips glistening. She had coaxed her young friend through her first small orgasm. It had been remarkably easy to achieve, and she did it with great care, aiming to whet the pretty blonde's appetite rather than dull it.

Count de Tranville lifted himself from Madame Coubette. He craved a glass of wine and pulled his breeches up from around his ankles.

Finding the skirt he had ripped from the woman, he noted that he had indeed torn it. She would be unable to wear it again without careful repair.

Her verbal attacks on Elise were not new, but they always annoyed him. From finding his charge involved with his pretty kitchen maid, he knew that a wild spirit lurked within the beautiful girl.

But how could Madame Coubette know of this? Women's intuition, he concluded. But could other people also sense Elise's dark nature? And what sort of gossip might his mistress be spreading? It was her insinuations that there was something between him and Elise that worried him most, however... and now between him and Genevieve, too. It was hard enough resisting the temptation of the two youthful beauties, without having to listen to intimations from the fiercely jealous woman. Anger mixed with disdain as he gazed down at her bare posterior. He would need to get a maid to fix her skirt before she went home.

Madame Coubette was still an attractive woman, but she was becoming an increasing irritant. The sensuous woman who had enchanted him a year before was fading, and a frightful shrew was replacing her.

Of course he might enjoy other women in Portugal, or wherever, but what did it have to do with her? He mentally admonished himself for allowing the married whore to feel she could be something akin to his wife. It was not wise. Should he have invited her on the trip with him? Probably not. No, definitely not, he decided. In fact, it was probably time to get rid of her.

Madame Coubette stirred and stood up, somewhat unsteadily. 'Put this on and then go up to Elise's room and find something to wear so I can get it repaired,' he suggested, passing her the damaged skirt. 'It is too damaged to go home in. Tell Elise you had an accident of some kind. I'm sure she'll find you something of hers to wear, and I can then get someone to mend it.'

'I can't come to Portugal, you know that, don't you?' she said firmly, putting on and fastening the skirt. 'And if you do go, we probably won't see each other again.'

'I'll be back,' he said determinedly. 'Once this madness is over, I will return.'

'Don't make idle promises. You'll never keep them.'

'We're living in terrible times. Times that call for sacrifices of one kind or another. I've asked you to come with me. I will already be sacrificing my home and country because I have no choice. You have a choice and it's best that you consider it well.'

'I have given you over a year of my life. You have given me nothing in return and now you take leave of me as if I were?'

'Just consider my predicament and consider my offer,' the count interrupted, losing his patience.

'No,' his mistress hissed back, surprising him with her vehemence, 'you consider my offer. You will stay here in France and there will be no more mention of leaving. If you go there will be trouble. I'll get you arrested before you leave.'

Genevieve still tingled all over. Though feeling shy, she felt a warm delight in her near nakedness. She felt so vulnerable and yet so free, too. She wanted Elise to touch her again, to repeat what she had just done.

But Elise was now beside the bed, holding the curtain cords. 'Stand up,' she ordered. 'It's time for your next lesson.'

Without thinking Genevieve obeyed again, a feeling of lightness permeating her body. Elise made her turn her back, stroked the girl's long blonde hair, and then pulled her arms behind her.

'Lovers play games, Genevieve,' she whispered. 'And a man's game is essentially that of power.'

Genevieve trembled a little, feeling the thick cord being wound and knotted tightly around her wrists. What was her friend up to now?

'Wuh-what are you doing?' she asked.

'As I said, it is time for your next lesson. A lesson in power and control.' Elise lifted the second cord. 'Now open your mouth,' she ordered.

Partly in fear, partly in fascination, Genevieve complied and felt the cord passing over her lips and lodging between her teeth. Elise tied it behind her head, forming a gag. 'Now get on your knees,' she commanded, pushing her to the floor.

Genevieve did as she was told, but Elise pushed her further so that her head sank forward and rested on the soft bed. She fidgeted apprehensively, a sudden panic gripping her, aware of her exposure and complete vulnerability.

'Relax,' Elise murmured, her hand following the delicious shape of Genevieve's bottom. 'Now, power is a man's favourite thing, and learning to submit to the whims of others is part of the lesson you must learn. Men love whores and slaves, and you must learn to become a whore and a slave if you want to win their affections.'

The hand withdrew, and then suddenly slapped Genevieve sharply on her buttocks. She swallowed the shriek of shock and pain that tried to force itself through the gag. Heat surged through her bottom as if she'd been scalded.

'What a man's pleasures are might not always be understandable to you, but learning to enjoy them is the challenge,' Elise said, stroking Genevieve's bottom again, but just as the kneeling girl felt the pain subsiding a second swipe fizzed through the air, the slap landing on her right buttock. It scorched more than the first, sending a raging heat over the surface of her skin and resonating deeply.

Tears welled in her eyes. She pulled at the cord in vain, but along with the pain, she realised, came the pleasurable throbbing Elise's tongue had only just partially abated. Her pussy was tingling again, warming and dampening. The pain in her buttocks mingled with it, inflaming it like a fan. She spread her knees discreetly wider, preparing to receive the next slap.

A zing resounded with the slap of a taut palm against the lower curve of her buttocks, making her writhe once more. The scalding sensation spread further. Something was welling up inside amid the pain and humiliation.

Elise noted the surreptitious movement of the lovely girl's knees, and sniggered. 'So, now the mare is hungry to be fucked,' she goaded. 'But not yet.'

Taking Genevieve by the shoulders she lifted her so that she was once more upright on her knees. She loosened the gag so that it slipped down around her neck and stepped before the girl. Her cool hands cupped Genevieve's flushed face, and she sat on the warm spot just vacated by the kneeling girl. 'That was the second part of today's lesson,' she told her plaything. 'And now for the third.'

Elise brushed aside the blonde fringe from Genevieve's damp brow, and the kneeling girl gazed at Elise's taut stomach and the dark triangle of curls nestled between her parted thighs. The sitting girl rubbed the glistening lips hiding there, and without a word she slowly parted them, her fingertips locating her clitoris.

'You have now seen the toy men have between their legs,' she said huskily, her free hand stroking Genevieve's hair. 'This is ours, and it needs to be kissed and adored. Kiss it for me, my dear Genevieve.'

Genevieve looked up into her friend's eyes, and then down to the moist, beckoning pussy before her. She closed her eyes and moved her face tentatively to the moist lips. Nervously she ran her tongue over the damp and fragrant flesh, but instantly felt her face being pressed deeper, urged by the hands of her friend. She felt wetness spreading over her lips, nose, and cheeks. Elise moaned. 'That's it,' she encouraged dreamily. 'That's it.' She took Genevieve's head in her hands and guided her mouth over her clitoris. With fingers urgently entwined in Genevieve's hair she bared her pleasure button to the girl with the other hand. Genevieve tongued it obediently, conscious now of the extent of the pleasure Elise was experiencing...

A noise suddenly startled them both. Genevieve tried to withdraw, to see what was happening, but a fierce swat and intense pain erupted on her bottom once more and she yelped loudly. Tears blurred her vision. Elise had not moved, but shock was etched on her face.

'I told you so!' Madame Coubette gloated.

'Silence!' the count thundered, his glazed eyes giving him the countenance of a madman. 'This is not Elise's doing,' he growled at his mistress in defence of his stepdaughter, with a display of bullish conviction he didn't actually believe. 'I can't be.' He glared at Genevieve. 'What on earth are you doing to my stepdaughter? Both of you will be punished tomorrow morning,' he went on to Elise before poor Genevieve could even think of a response, let alone impart one, 'giving you time between now and then to dwell on your disgraceful behaviour. Bring her at ten o'clock sharp. You know where!'

Elise stood and hastily untied the cord around Genevieve's wrists. He watched them for a moment, and then left with Madame Coubette in his trail, who looked back at Elise and smiled...

# Chapter Three

Genevieve's legs were trembling as she followed Elise into the library. She had never been in there before. It was the count's preserve and out of bounds. Her eyes flitted over the book-lined walls of the austere room, alighting on a portrait hanging over the large fireplace of a beautiful dark-haired woman.

The fire was lit, and the count paced to and fro before it, his hands behind his back. To the left of the fireplace was his writing desk and chair, and to the right was a leather armchair.

Elise seemed very composed, surprising Genevieve. Perhaps there was nothing much to fear, after all.

The count turned to face them, and Elise stopped just in front of him. She stood proudly, mirroring his stance, her hands behind her back, her shoulders set proudly. Genevieve took her place beside her, and on the armchair she noticed a leather riding-crop with a loop at the tip.

The count wore no wig, and she observed his short greying hair and brown eyes, seeking some trace of compassion. But there was none to be found, his stare cold with determination.

Genevieve stole a sideways glance at Elise, who still seemed to be in perfect control of her emotions. How could she be so calm and collected?

'I find it hard to believe that one of the de Montvert stock could turn out to be such a depraved little hussy,' the count said to Genevieve. 'You have brought depravity to my home and corrupted the girl I have raised as my own for seven years.'

Genevieve couldn't believe the unjust severity of the charge. Her heart began thumping as she vainly sought some way of explaining what the count had witnessed without blaming Elise. But her guardian turned away from her and addressed his stepdaughter.

'You know what to expect,' he said.

Genevieve heard a rustle and looked at Elise, shocked as the girl unbuttoned her bodice and removed her clothes.

'You should be ashamed of yourself for allowing this wretch to corrupt you in such a way,' he went on. 'As you know, there is only one way to deal with this sort of disgraceful behaviour.'

The count turned again to Genevieve. 'Take off your clothes, too,' he ordered, and a wave of panic flooded her, a hot flush colouring her cheeks. 'And hurry up about it!'

The poor girl reddened and anxiously began fumbling with the buttons of her bodice. Elise, meanwhile, was already naked, the fire dancing on her creamy thighs. Her proud breasts swayed firmly as she kicked her dress and underwear to one side, and moved to the armchair.

Not wanting to incur the count's wrath any more than she already had, Genevieve hastened to undress too. Despite the heat of the fire she shivered and crossed her arms over her breasts, her nipples hardening.

The count manoeuvred the armchair to face the fireplace, and then the writing desk too.

'Over the chair with you, Elise,' he instructed, and his stepdaughter bent gracefully, her hands placed firmly on its arms as she bent over its back.

Gazing at the shapely buttocks, Genevieve could make out the pink cleft of her sex, the same wet lips she had been introduced to the day before, causing all this trouble now. It glistened with moisture, inviting her...

Count de Tranville held the crop. He lifted his arm, and then brought it down with a sharp sweep across Elise's bottom. Genevieve's heart jumped at the sound of the assault, and she watched as her friend's lovely bottom twitched in a brief spasm at the impact. She looked in horror at a burning red line striping Elise's poor buttocks. A second strike followed, sweeping down with the same ferocity. This time a faint yelp came from the bent girl as her buttocks quivered again.

'Enough,' the count panted after administering a third cruel swat.

Elise raised herself slowly from her position. Her face glowed red and perspiration beaded her forehead.

Genevieve gazed at the girl's heaving breasts and then tried to cast a look of sympathy to her, but Elise's shining eyes turned immediately to the count. He turned to face Genevieve.

'Now you,' he said. 'Take her place over the armchair.'

Genevieve felt her legs trembling almost uncontrollably, but the pulsing rhythm was between her thighs again. She couldn't move.

'I knew a little hussy like you would have problems taking her medicine,' Count de Tranville said, then without warning he grabbed her wrist and as she squealed an incoherent protest he pressed her facedown across the desk instead.

'No!' Genevieve managed to shriek, shaking with chagrin, her cheeks aflame. Tears welled in her eyes and she struggled to raise herself, but a sharp push from the count pressed her back down on the desktop, and his hand remained between her shoulders, pinning her to the polished surface.

'Hold her hands,' Count de Tranville ordered Elise, and she obediently grasped Genevieve's wrists and pulled them to the desk's edge. Speechlessly Genevieve searched her friend's eyes for some empathy, and was shocked to find none. Her buttocks, exposed to the count, suddenly felt chilly and unbearably vulnerable. What was he doing behind her...?

The vicious leather crop whistled through the air and sank into Genevieve's buttocks, making her howl as it scorched a path across them and made her squirm frantically against the hands holding her. She had never been punished so severely in her young life before, but the pain in her bottom, far from being unbearable, was fanning the delicious heat already simmering there.

27

# Chapter Four

When Elise told Genevieve that Rodolfo was a man who could not be content with just one woman, she could hardly have been more right, and he would have been the first to confess this. Nature had bestowed Rodolfo with gifts that many men would envy. He was rich, handsome, and possessed an athletic frame. He was also very well endowed.

But, while Rodolfo was a man to delight many a woman in bed, he had also grown difficult to satisfy. He had enjoyed sleeping with so many in Portugal, Spain and France, that at the age of twenty-five an ennui began to affect him. So to rectify this he had taken to experimenting with other practices.

Wild parties in Paris took his fancy for a while, but he eventually grew tired of them. And while from time to time even men offered themselves to his curiosity, he never really felt much interest in such a departure. So currently he found contentment sleeping with a number of pretty women at the same time, usually in the better Parisian brothels.

It was for these reasons that when Rodolfo awoke in his apartment in Paris, naked beneath his goose feather quilt, he was not startled to feel the warmth and weight of two soft bodies moulding against him. He threw back the quilt and stared at the two girls sprawled beside him, and it took a moment to recall their names - Claudine and Juliette, that was it.

Both were blonde, and whilst Claudine was naked Juliette slept in her black corset. Claudine, the slighter of the two, rested her head on his stomach, while Juliette nestled in the crook of his arm.

Claudine and Juliette, he mused... the young and destitute former mistresses of an executed aristocrat. He had found them in a Paris brothel, and taken by the beauty of the fallen pair, so totally at odds with the shabby den in which they resided, he took them home with him.

It was strange how similar the two were. They had almost the same shade of blonde hair; their skin had a similar olive hue, and there was not that much difference in their shape or size.

It was lucky for them that he found them only recently after they started working in the seedy brothel, before the delicacy of their beauty had been completely erased by their labours among the grubby hands and lusty loins of countless miserly commoners.

What a state France was in, he contemplated, and then his thoughts drifted to his visit to the Count de Tranville.

At first deep reluctance had filled him when he received his father's instruction to assist the count in fleeing the country. But the sight of the man's two beautiful charges quickly changed his mind. What was there to keep him in Paris, anyway?

And what a treat Elise had turned out to be! And Genevieve... he was sure he had never seen such a beautiful girl before. Thoughts of the two made him stir, and he looked at the two sleeping girls beside him. What was he to do with them? When they were not making love, the two were the best servants he'd ever had. Neither complained of anything, and both did whatever they were told.

Then it occurred to him to take them with him. But what would he tell Count de Tranville and his father? Why, he would introduce them as yet more imperilled aristocrats whom he was gallantly rescuing. Claudine could be the countess of somewhere, Juliette the baroness of somewhere else. Splendid!

Having made the decision he relaxed into his pillows and smiled. Yes, it would be too great a shame to leave France without them.

After the thrashing received from the count, Genevieve fled to her bedchamber in tears. The punishment left her perplexed and at a loss to understand her own feelings. She felt fury at her guardian for being so unfair and so brutal, but at the same time she acknowledged the pleasure the blows had awoken.

Her feelings toward Elise similarly confused her. On the one hand she resented the assistance she'd given him in the administration of the punishment - a punishment far more protracted than the one Elise had to endure, and a punishment for which Elise had been responsible in the first place - but on the other hand the memories of the pleasures she'd experienced earlier at her hand remained.

The following day Elise complained of a headache and asked for her meals to be brought to her bedroom. She also issued instructions that she was not to be disturbed by anyone, including Genevieve.

Genevieve felt despair at the announcement. What was the matter with her friend and why couldn't she visit her? She began to feel lonely. She breakfasted alone and wondered what to do for the rest of the day, hoping Elise might feel better as it wore on.

But as the afternoon came Elise still had not emerged, and glumly Genevieve decided to take a walk alone. Without a fixed itinerary she wandered across the lawns and headed for the woods beyond. A path cut through the trees and she followed it for some time.

She soon began to relax. It was lovely in the woods, and the singing birds and the rustle of the wind through branches lulled her. Her thoughts slowly returned to Elise and then to Rodolfo.

It now seemed so long since she had seen the man. It was difficult to remember just how he looked. Especially after the games she had played with Elise.

The dark hair and powerful eyes of the man and her friend merged, so that Rodolfo suddenly loomed in her mind like a sorceress and Elise became a dashing foreign gentlemen. She would see Rodolfo again soon, though, she remembered.

What would he feel for her? Would a man capable of so casually doing what he had done with Elise be capable of ever loving her? And would she please him? After all, what did she really have to offer? Nothing any more, except her heart and love.

Genevieve came across a rutted road cutting through the woods, and caught sight of a small house. She had walked for quite some time now, and was beginning to feel tired and thirsty. Perhaps the occupants would allow her a drink and a little time to rest.

But from first impressions the house appeared to be deserted. Slightly nervously she tapped on its heavy oak door, but there was no reply. Again she knocked, harder this time, but again there was no reply. She waited for a minute or so before deciding that there was probably nobody there, but just as she turned away the door creaked open.

'Can I help you, mademoiselle?' a soft voice asked.

Genevieve turned back to see a young blonde girl of about her age standing before her.

'Is everything all right, mademoiselle?' the girl asked.

'Yes,' Genevieve replied, after a pause, slightly taken aback by the loveliness of the girl. 'I've been walking in the woods for a long time and was wondering if I could perhaps ask for a drink to quench my thirst.'

'Of course you can,' the girl chimed sweetly, a bright smile lighting up her clear face. 'Please, come in.'

As Genevieve accepted the invitation she remained quiet, for there was something about the girl that fascinated her. She could hardly take her eyes from her lovely face.

Sitting at the scrubbed table, Genevieve watched the girl fetch her a drink of milk, and kindly place a plate of bread and cheese before her too, noting how quiet the house was and sensing the girl was its only resident.

As Genevieve enjoyed the frugal but tasty snack and cool drink she gazed at the surroundings. It was obviously not a prosperous place. The wooden floorboards were clean but loose and in need of repair, and the walls had evidently not been painted for many years. On a few hooks there were dusty traps and snares that had clearly not been used for a long time and now served as ornaments.

She thanked the girl warmly for the refreshment and gazed at her, taken with her good looks despite her worn, woollen skirt that had been patched many times. It was probably the only one the girl had. Quietly, the girl took a mop and began cleaning the floor, but the worn skirt and blouse did not hide altogether what was obviously a shapely and beautiful body beneath. And then it dawned on Genevieve why she was so fascinated by the girl; there was something peculiarly familiar about her, like looking at herself. They could be mistaken for sisters or cousins, Genevieve realised. They had the same soft features, the same light blonde hair, and the same pale blue eyes. Her figure, slim and graceful, was like hers too. Even her voice had the same soft ring. Genevieve felt a deep fondness for the girl.

'Why is it so quiet here,' she asked, still watching the girl. 'There's not a soul around. Do you live here all by yourself?'

'I do, yes.' The girl stopped mopping, and with an innocent smile turned to Genevieve. 'Many have left this area, with it being so close to the Tranville chateau. The word is that the revolutionaries could call on the count at any time, and who knows what would happen to him, or to anyone thought to be a friend to him.'

It was true, it dawned on Genevieve. She had been so lost in her friendship with Elise and life at the chateau that she hadn't really noticed the gradually thinning local population.

Why was her guardian's home so empty? It had not seemed so at first, when she arrived there. But where were all the servants? She ran through those remaining in her mind; the elderly cook, two old maids that doubled as chambermaids, the old man she occasionally saw walking horses early in the morning... so few for such a large place. There was a coachman too, but even he was aged. Why, the place was almost empty apart from these ageing, quiet spectres.

And what of the revolution that was tearing up the country and that had taken her family? At the chateau it seemed not to be going on at all. Within the sturdy old building there was hardly ever mention of it, neither from her guardian or Elise.

The fear of it, if it existed, could only be apparent in the emptiness of their world and the absence of those who might otherwise share it. Since the visit of Rodolfo, the count had entertained no other guests, save Madame Coubette.

The girl's large eyes sparkled brightly and her face glowed pink. Genevieve gazed at her mouth, her teeth pearly white and neat, and when she talked she would occasionally moisten her lips with a darting glide of her tongue.

'I am alone now,' the girl went on. 'My husband left me not long ago. This place was his, and he left it to me. So, I suppose I should be grateful to him for that. Anyway, he drank too much, and he said I didn't love him enough. He didn't think there was any future for him here. He said he might come back one day, but I doubt it.'

Pity for the girl suddenly mingled with Genevieve's affection. 'But you're so young to be on your own,' she said. 'I would never have imagined you to be married. Why, you can't be any older than me. Do you miss him?'

'No,' the girl replied, shaking her head. 'I didn't love him. It was a mistake from the start.'

'Then why did you marry him?'

'I had liked him at first, though I soon regretted it,' the girl replied matter-of-factly. 'There was little choice after I lost my job at the chateau, though.'

'You worked there?' Genevieve asked, surprised by the news.

'Only for a short time,' the girl muttered slowly. 'I was a kitchen maid.'

'And what happened?' Genevieve asked.

'Well, the count took me on as a kitchen maid, but I soon found out that he had other things in mind. He's a distinguished man, and was very kind to me, and one day, as I brought him his breakfast, he made his fondness for me very clear. I'm sure he would have carried on being kind to me, if it wasn't for Mademoiselle Elise.'

At the mention of Elise, Genevieve felt her heart quicken and her curiosity sharpen. The name caused something to stir in the blonde girl, too, she saw. She seemed suddenly to be on the verge of tears. 'What do you mean?' Genevieve probed.

'Elise...' the girl sighed. 'She took an interest in me. Almost from the start. She played all sorts of games with my heart. Games that were cruel and that I didn't understand. At times it was wonderful, but at other times I felt she was wicked through and through... but she won my heart.'

The girl seemed lost. A tear trickled down her cheek, and she wiped it away quickly with her sleeve.

'Are you trying to tell me that you were... were *lovers?*' Genevieve asked, aghast, staring deeply into the girl's damp eyes.

The blonde maid looked back wistfully at Genevieve. 'At first I thought we were, yes,' she admitted. 'But for some reason Elise soon stopped being my lover and became cruel and distant.'

The girl stared down at her feet and then looked back up at Genevieve. 'In any case,' she continued, 'the count put a stop to it and sent me away. I was penniless and alone until I met my husband. It's probably just as well, because the chateau is a scary place. They say the ghosts of his wife and his ancestors haunt it. I suppose I'm lucky to be out of there.'

'Oh,' Genevieve said absently, 'but it's since become my only home.'

'Then, I'd urge you to be careful,' the girl advised, stepping closer and putting her hand on Genevieve's shoulder. 'If I may say so, you are very beautiful, and seem to be kind of heart too. That place is dangerous, I think. Dangerous for you.'

It was getting late and Genevieve realised she needed to be making her way home. 'Can I come back and see you?' she asked, realising how much she had enjoyed the brief time she'd spent with the girl.

'Of course, mademoiselle,' the girl beamed, brightening up at the prospect of having some occasional company, 'I would be very happy for you to visit me.'

'And I don't yet know your name?' Genevieve prompted.

'It's Emelie, mademoiselle,' the girl told her.

'Emelie,' Genevieve echoed. 'That's a lovely name.' She smiled at the girl. 'And don't call me mademoiselle,' she said gently. 'My name is Genevieve.

'Now, I'd better be going.'

'It's getting colder outside, I think,' the girl said, peering out through one of the small windows. 'I'm going to light a fire soon and prepare a broth. Are you sure you wouldn't like to stay for the night? There is room for you.'

Genevieve gazed into the girl's eyes thoughtfully. How pretty they were. 'No, thank you,' she responded. 'They would wonder where I was. Another time, perhaps.'

'Then perhaps you might like to borrow a cloak to take with you.'

Genevieve accepted the thoughtful offer and Emelie hurried to another room, returning with a heavy woollen mantel and wrapping it tenderly around Genevieve's shoulders.

'What fine hair you have,' she said, gently pushing back the golden locks of Genevieve's hair over the collar of the cloak. Affectionately Genevieve took Emelie's hands as she finished fastening the cloak at her throat, without thinking she kissed the girl's cheek, and as she did the girl turned her face and met her lips with her own.

Emelie gave the kiss intimately, with her eyes closed, and as Genevieve's mouth lingered on hers, she subconsciously allowed her lips to part, surprised to feel Emelie's tongue grazing hers. It probed nervously and she allowed it to roam inquisitively for a few seconds, as if to signal that the unusual response to her farewell kiss had been noted, her heartbeat quickening.

Then, reluctantly pulling away, Genevieve gazed at the girl. 'I really must be going now, but I'll come again soon,' she whispered.

'Be careful,' Emelie called, standing at her front door, waving as Genevieve set off on her way.

The trace of the girl's lips remained with Genevieve as she walked quickly through the woods. It was getting chilly, but she felt gratefully warm beneath the cloak. What a lovely new friend she had found. The memory of Emelie's prettiness and soft nature made her smile. It would have been so delightfully cosy to remain there.

She pictured herself sitting by a warm fire next to the girl, chatting into the night. Then she thought of the kiss again. What had inspired her to do something like that with a stranger, and to let the stranger return her kiss like she had?

Then for a moment she felt like turning back, but she feared her hosts at the chateau would worry about her absence.

Much of what Emelie had said left her worried and curious, though. What if it were true that the revolutionaries could descend on the chateau and arrest them at any time?

And what about the experiences the girl had been through at the hands of the count and his stepdaughter? She remembered the count's erect member as Madame Coubette knelt at his feet, and tried to imagine him doing the same to fair Emelie as she took him his breakfast.

And what had Elise done to her that still seemed to haunt her so? It had sounded as if Elise had been very cruel indeed.

Was Elise trying to do the same to her now? Had she decided to make her Emelie's replacement? If so, what sort of fate awaited her? But whatever was to be, it appeared she had found a new friend, she reflected.

Before she knew it, it was getting towards dusk and she decided to increase her pace. The singing of the birds had been replaced by other less familiar and somewhat disconcerting sounds, and she wanted to get home. This time she kept to the road, and after a little while she heard a noise behind her and turned to see a coach and horses approaching, and she recognised it at once as Madame Coubette's.

The prospect of meeting the woman again was not in the least bit welcome, for she recalled how the woman was present when the count discovered her and Elise together. There was, however, little chance of avoiding the coach.

It soon caught up and halted, the near door swinging open. 'Why, if it isn't the fair young Genevieve,' crowed Madame Coubette. 'What are you doing out here by yourself?'

'I was just taking a walk,' Genevieve replied shyly, 'but I got a little distracted and didn't realise how late it's getting.' She didn't see any reason to tell the woman about her new friend.

Madame Coubette wore a brocaded gold dress, studded here and there with bright stones. It was cut low to reveal her ample cleavage, and on the generous upper slope of one breast Genevieve could see a small tattooed design that, at a glance, looked like a star. Above her powdered visage the woman wore her usual white wig. 'Don't you know it's not safe for you to be out here alone any more?' she said. 'It's getting dark and cold, too. Come, get in and ride with me. I'm on my way to the chateau to see the count.'

Genevieve found herself blushing as she climbed up; what could she say after spying the spectacle of the woman and the count? And what would Madame Coubette be thinking after witnessing the shameful spectacle of her and Elise together?

'I hope the count did not punish you too severely yesterday morning,' the woman said without preamble. 'He often has too quick and hot a temper, and a heavy hand.' Genevieve remained silent, sitting beside Madame Coubette. 'Perhaps,' the woman continued, 'your pretty little derrière is still sore. Like most men, he does not understand we ladies.' She casually laid a hand on Genevieve's knee and squeezed. 'He's lucky that I understand him, though. That's why we're such close friends, despite our backgrounds.'

Coyly, Genevieve glanced at the woman. She radiated an elegant voluptuousness. It was enticing and yet daunting. She thought how she had at times heard talk of courtesans and women of pleasure, and though she had never met any, she imagined they would be something not so far removed from the ornate woman beside her.

Madame Coubette returned the inspection, her look indecipherable and invasive, and it made Genevieve lower her eyes.

'Don't be so shy of me, my darling,' the woman chided. 'Your little liaison with Elise seems perfectly charming to me. We girls have all sorts of passions of which men know nothing. There are things we can share with each other that men simply don't understand. Men have created the world and they are the masters of it. It is for this reason that we must please them. We are their toys and we learn how to make them happy. But when it comes to our pleasures... oh, it is so often only another woman that understands.'

Madame Coubette moved closer to Genevieve and the hand on her knee massaged gently, making Genevieve uncomfortable. 'I-I don't understand what you mean,' she stuttered defensively. 'And I think you may have the wrong idea; Elise and I are good friends and we were only playing a game.'

'Oh, of course you were,' the woman mocked, her eyes sparkling mischievously. 'But tell me, are you just Elise's whore, or are you available to outside offers too?' Genevieve couldn't believe her ears, but the woman went on before she could relay her indignation. 'I mean, do you have a going rate? A list of services offered, perhaps?' Anger gripped Genevieve, but she was rendered utterly speechless by the woman's outrageous musings. 'How much would you charge, for example, to provide a little tongue work on a lady like me?'

The hand on Genevieve's knee moved and clamped through her dress between her thighs, the fingers finding and latching to the lips of her sex, and the harsh assault sent a bewildering, unexpected tremor through her.

Then with the poor girl stunned and distracted by the speed and unexpectedness of the assault, the woman gripped her blonde hair with her free hand and tugged back, arching Genevieve's slender neck and making her squeal at the vicious discomfort, involuntarily thrusting her breasts forward.

Madame Coubette's countenance was now extremely alarming as she undid the rough cloak around Genevieve's shoulders and gazed hungrily down at her bare throat and cleavage. The girl's breasts swelled as she breathed anxiously, her tight bodice rendering their creamy upper slopes available to the woman's greedy eyes.

'It is best that you know and understand this well, my little orphaned slut,' the woman whispered harshly, her face close to Genevieve's. 'As far as your guardian is concerned, I am his mistress and the only mistress and lady of the de Tranville estate. I am all he could want, and I have been as close to being his wife as any woman will ever be. I have worked hard to make it that way, so you're whoring in the wrong place.'

Genevieve stared at Madame Coubette in utter shock.

'And if you're going to try and curry favour with anyone, you'd do well to start with me and stop your little pussy-kissing games with Elise. With her you are wasting your time, but I will teach and reward you.'

'Let go of me!' Genevieve suddenly found her voice. 'You are the whore, not me!' She shook her head to try and dislodge the fingers gripping her roots, only succeeding in increasing the sharp pain. But Madame Coubette merely cackled her amusement at the futile mini-rebellion, and feeling the struggling girl's warmth through her dress, she thrust her hand even harder against it.

'You're *very* ripe,' she mocked. 'You see, we're going to get on very well together.'

'Let go of me!' Genevieve yelled again, but the arrogant woman merely laughed and clamped her mouth to her exposed throat, while increasing the pressure between her legs even more. Genevieve could feel the woman's fingers probing insistently, trying to press the cloth of her dress and underwear into her. She squirmed desperately, trying to get free of the hold despite the pain it caused her.

'Please, leave me alone, I want to get out,' she begged desperately, trying to lean away from the lips that devoured her throat and were moving down towards her cleavage.

'Very well,' the woman said, taking her by surprise, and with two taps on the ceiling she ordered the coachman to stop, whereupon Genevieve was surprised to see they weren't too far from the chateau, 'if that's what you think you want. But this is only a temporary reprieve. I will have you, believe me.'

Genevieve opened the coach door and stepped down quickly, slamming it behind her.

'Remember what I've said, my precious little thing,' Madame Coubette called as the coach moved off again. 'I know your game, and as a novice, you'd be better off with an experienced agent like me.'

# Chapter Five

The day following her punishment Elise brooded in her room, but it was not the beating itself that bothered her. In fact, the experience delighted her.

When the second stroke of the count's crop had sizzled on her bottom Genevieve gasped with pity at the tremors that ran over Elise's chastised buttocks. But, unknown to the innocent girl, the tremors were not a result of pain. With that blow a gentle orgasm had flooded Elise, which she was straining to conceal.

But pain in itself was not a particularly enjoyable experience for Elise; it was the touch of the count's wrath and the strike of his anger on her body that had become a delicacy for her.

The only disconsolation was that his actions went no further. She had bared herself to him that day as seductively as she could, fully aware of her allure and suspecting how much lust it truly evoked in him. She recognised her own sultry voluptuousness, and knew that few who saw it could fail to be stirred, but she remained the fruit he would not touch and it had rendered her frustrated for so long.

Elise recalled how enjoyable it had been to see her lovely friend writhing tearfully, her beaten bottom so adorably pink and blotchy. Genevieve, so pretty but so, so naïve, she mused.

No, the beating had not been bad at all, but what did continue to rankle were the things Madame Coubette had said about her. The woman seemed to be aware of her frustrations concerning her stepfather, and she also seemed aware of other things about Elise. Why else had she called her a whore?

Elise bathed in the afternoon and then dozed, and when she awoke it was to the sound of a coach approaching. At first she assumed it was her stepfather returning from his trip into town, but she gazed down from her window and was surprised to see Madame Coubette's coach again. What was she doing returning so soon after her last visit?

Madame Coubette would be disappointed because the count had not returned yet, and a calculating smile lifted the corners of Elise's mouth. She would go down to greet the woman, she decided.

She dressed quickly and went down to the drawing room, her hands behind her back, her chest thrust out. One of the few remaining maids opened the front door and Madame Coubette entered the drawing room with her usual flamboyant grace, but her smile wilted as she saw Elise and not the count.

'Good evening,' the sultry girl welcomed her.

'Elise, how nice to see you again,' the woman said tightly. 'But where is your stepfather?'

'He clearly wasn't aware that you were visiting today, and he's gone into town.' Elise smiled coolly. 'I'm afraid he won't be back until late.'

'What a shame,' Madame Coubette said, the atmosphere between them strained.

'Indeed,' Elise concurred for false civility. 'And I am sure he'll be tired out when he returns.'

Madame Coubette looked coldly at Elise. The young woman filled her with wrath, a feeling so strong that she struggled to suppress it. But she knew how much the count seemed to care for his stepdaughter, and calculated it would not be wise to be too openly hostile to the girl. 'I came to discuss his proposal to leave the country,' she stated. 'I think he might need to think it through a little more carefully.'

'I doubt he would have mentioned it if he hadn't thought it through,' Elise replied tartly. Increasing anger gripped the woman and Elise recognised it, making her bolder. 'You don't like me very much, do you, Madame Coubette?' she goaded.

'Why, my dear girl, I don't know what you mean,' the woman countered coldly.

Elise stared at her accusatorily for a few moments. 'Well, the last time you were sucking my stepfather's cock you called me a whore,' Elise stated dryly. 'I would hardly call that a term of endearment.'

The smile Madame Coubette had managed to hold thus far evaporated instantly. How boldly Elise had cast the gauntlet at her! 'Perhaps the count would have enjoyed having you kneeling where I was,' she hissed back, her eyes narrowing vehemently. 'And I know you would happily have knelt in my place.' Elise stared at her blankly, taken aback for a moment. 'Oh yes, there is much I know about you, young lady. Do you think these old walls have no ears, or that they keep your mischief silent? And what have you been up to with your delicious young friend?'

Elise struggled to construct a reply, whilst Madame Coubette scented blood and went for the jugular.

'Oh yes, the little morsel looks like quite a tasty treat. So much so that I would not say no to a bite of her myself.' The woman licked her lips salaciously, enjoying the ease with which she'd snatched the upper hand from Elise. 'But tell me,' she went on, driving home her advantage, 'didn't you know that silence has a price? Why, there's a revolutionary committee in town that would love to hear tales of depraved aristocratic households like this one... and depraved aristocrats trying to flee the country, too.'

Madame Coubette was gloating. The gauntlet had been skilfully thrown back and Elise, though still relatively composed, was struggling to pick it up again.

'And what sort of *price* does this *silence* cost?' she asked, but with little conviction.

'I'll need to give it some thought,' the woman said triumphantly. 'Tell the count I paid him a visit and that I need to talk to him urgently about his proposed departure.'

Madame Coubette rose. 'I will leave now, but consider closely what I have said...'

'Tell me, Madame Coubette,' Elise said hastily, 'how does your husband feel about your visits to the count? And how does the revolutionary committee feel about aristocrats' whores?'

Madame Coubette smiled knowingly at Elise and sat back down. 'My husband knows about my visits to the count and doesn't mind in the least,' she explained, patronisingly. 'And as for the revolutionary committee, well, I've been a whore and a procuress for them and their friends for quite a while. So they wouldn't care too much, either. I'm one of the people, Elise, and you are not, and that's all that matters to them. They love me and they hate you. Good try, though.'

Madame Coubette again looked thoughtfully at Elise. 'You know,' she went on, 'I may not like you, young lady, nor you me, but the more I talk to you the more I find we have in common. You remind me of myself when I was younger, although when I was about your age I married my husband. He was a businessman and moneylender, older than me, already balding and losing his teeth when we wed. My father owed him a lot of money and settled some of his debt by offering him me. I was beautiful then, strong and fiery, like you. But my husband didn't want me just for that. He knew that a desirable girl would be a good investment, if used and managed properly. And that's what he did. My beauty has helped make us rich and powerful. It has been enjoyed by whomever he knew might be useful to him. And now my husband is old, and not much longer for this world.'

Elise contemplated the woman opposite her with growing interest... and possibly even begrudging admiration.

'I've slept with so many wealthy trades people and aristocrats,' Madame Coubette continued. 'That's how most of my time was spent at your age. It was strange, I was young and so beautiful and all of them were old and so self-important.'

Coubette began chuckling to herself. 'There was one time, only six months after we married, that my husband owed money to a shipping company whose founder lived in Rency. He spent a week in protracted discussions with the old man. Anyway, my husband told me that for the next month I was to visit the old lecher each Thursday night and not return until Friday afternoon. He instructed that I was to do whatever he asked, no matter how strange it seemed.'

Elise was amazed by what she was hearing.

'So, there I would be,' the surprising woman continued, 'travelling to that huge house on a Thursday evening, terrified. But before the man even touched me in bed he would fall asleep, muttering inanely to himself and then setting about snoring loud enough to wake the dead. In the end I got so fed up that I would wander around his cold house at night, wondering what to do, and then I ended up being seduced by his senior housemaid. She would make love to me for hours and then by morning I would creep back to his bed. When he woke up he would thank me for my time and kiss my forehead, completely unaware that we had done nothing intimate together. But at least the debt was forgotten.'

Madame Coubette began to look more wistful. 'I grew richer, yes,' she said, 'but love and true pleasure for me were never there. So many years later I even tried to buy love, like the men who bought their pleasures from me, but I never found it until I met the count. He is the man that was always meant for me. And the joining of our wealth... why, we would be so powerful in a new France.'

'But can't you see?' Elise said. 'The count cannot marry you. He can enjoy you, and perhaps even care for you, but no matter how many aristocrats you've slept with, or how good you are in bed, or how wealthy, you are not of noble blood. He can never marry you.'

A glaze of hatred possessed the woman's face, and Elise observed it pensively.

'It is just one of those things,' she concluded. 'And even if you were of noble blood, he would not marry you.'

Madame Coubette's brow wrinkled with confusion.

'He loved my mother too deeply,' the girl explained. 'She was a very desirable and passionate woman, and I think he sees the same in me. I think he secretly desires me, and this causes him much turmoil and plays heavily on his conscience.' She sighed reflectively. 'I am very much like my mother, in appearance and nature, and because of this I am sure my stepfather burns with passion when he looks at me. But he loved my mother deeply, and he wants to honour her in the way of nobles, so it is for this reason that he resists me. It is his way of honouring her, I think, and being noble.

'So he pretends I am just his wayward charge and tries his best to make a good lady of me, even though he burns with lust to have me as a mistress and feels deep down that trying to make a lady of me is futile. It is another of the foolish traits of the de Tranville blood, I suppose. So we are both unlucky.'

Madame Coubette pondered the girl's honest disclosure for a few minutes, and then said, 'You know, if Count de Tranville married me, it would be extremely convenient for both of you. I would not be a selfish or foolish woman. I know that as a man his eyes would wander and his passions might stray from time to time - especially with a beautiful girl like you at hand. What man could resist such temptation?'

Elise looked at her curiously.

'The world is changing,' Madame Coubette continued. 'Your stepfather is in grave danger because he is a noble and he believes in the old world. My husband is sick and not long for this world. By marrying me, a commoner, the count would be demonstrating his commitment to the cause of the revolution. Marriage with me would save him. He would not have to leave France. Together we could meet the committee and be a part of it. I know most of them. And he could show how he rejects the old regime, and how, through his marriage to me, he accepts the new one.'

'Hm... what you say sounds interesting,' Elise conceded.

'It is what I came here to discuss with him this evening,' Madame Coubette explained.

'Well, you'll need to discuss your idea with him very soon,' Elise pointed out. 'He's gone to town today to make the final arrangements for our departure to Portugal.'

Madame Coubette sighed, got up from her chair and sat beside Elise on the divan. She looked deeply at her and held her hands. 'Elise,' she said, 'we may not care too much for each other, but your world of nobility is over. Your class are being hounded and massacred. Soon there will be no more of you. There is no future for you here, and yes, you can run, but for what? A life in exile?'

Elise listened to the woman in silence. 'This is the only real plan that could save you,' she insisted. 'You are young and you clearly harbour desires toward the count. So be it. You are beautiful, but clearly as yet too inexperienced to know how to get what you want from a man. So I will teach you. I will help you capture your heart's desires.'

'But wouldn't you be jealous of me?' Elise asked.

'I want to marry your stepfather,' the woman insisted, 'that is all. It would be foolish to put him in a cage. But marrying me would leave him and his property safe forever. It would also provide him with not only a wife, but also a wise and consenting woman who already understands his needs, his desire for you, and your youthful fixation with him.'

Elise remained silent, lost in her thoughts, and during the pause both females heard Genevieve getting in and going straight upstairs to bed.

'It's strange,' Madame Coubette murmured, 'but I'm beginning to feel so much closer to you already. I know we could learn to share and live together peacefully. I can help you get what you want, Elise,' she added. 'But you must help me get what I want in return.'

'How?' Elise asked in hushed tones.

'You will make love to the count,' Madame Coubette revealed. 'I will be the one to arrange it. And then you will help to convince him of my plan, about how departure is foolish and why me must remain here to enjoy his wealth and my wealth and all kinds of pleasures.'

Elise absorbed the woman's words, and then nodded. 'It is best that you talk to my stepfather soon,' she said. 'This evening when he returns, or first thing tomorrow morning. You should stay here tonight. I will have the guestroom prepared.'

After Madame Coubette retired to her room Elise remained sitting for a while, her thoughts spinning with new plans and the hatching of new plans.

So Madame Coubette, the woman she had instinctively hated, was now her ally! Could her whore's plan work? Could the woman really serve to protect her and her stepfather from the revolution? And could she ensure that the silent passions that ran between him and her finally found an outlet?

The prospect had seemed dim until now, but Madame Coubette's guile and experience were beyond question, and if there was anyone who could help, it might be her after all...

Elise began thinking about Genevieve. How enjoyable it had felt bringing the beautiful girl to heel with her commands, and bringing her to the brink of her pleasures again. And, without doubt, Genevieve was beginning to love it, despite her coyness. Genevieve, as simple and beautiful as she was, was now her slave and it was simply her coyness that held her back.

After the count had punished them both in the library, he had detained Elise. She thought about how she stood before him, naked. He told her never to do what she had done with Genevieve again. What a strain his anger must have been for him; as she stood proudly before him she could not take her lowered eyes away from the prominent bulge thrusting from inside his breeches. And no doubt he could not have failed to observe what her eyes were observing.

But if the count made love to her while married to Madame Coubette, as the woman planned, how would Genevieve fit in?

Would the blossoming fun between her and her blonde friend be allowed to continue? Surely the hypocrisy would prove too great?

From the way the count had looked at Genevieve that day, and from the way Madame Coubette had looked at her upstairs in the bedchamber, it appeared that they too might want to indulge their own extraneous fantasies with the fair-haired beauty.

And what of it? Elise asked herself. If the count made her his woman, did anything else really matter?

Remembering the luscious vision of Genevieve tied and vulnerable over her bed made Elise stir, so she rose and went upstairs to the girl's bedroom, entering without knocking.

A solitary candle on a dresser opposite Genevieve's bed lit the room with a soft orange glow. Elise gazed at the white folds of sheets and could see the girl's blonde head buried in the pillows, her back turned to her as she approached.

'Are you awake?' Elise whispered.

Genevieve turned and sat up, and as she did so the sheet about her slid from her shoulders revealing her bare breasts. Elise contemplated them secretly. How comely they were...

'What do you want?' Genevieve muttered sleepily.

'I came to see how you are.'

'I'm fine,' Genevieve said shortly.

Elise slowly unbuttoned the bodice of her dress, and as she opened it her full breasts swayed firmly into view. Genevieve's eyes flitted over them, and standing before her, Elise dropped the dress to the floor. Genevieve gazed at Elise's body, shapely and alluring.

'What are you doing?' she whispered. 'If the count finds us like this again there'll be even more trouble for us.'

Elise ignored her comment, moving towards the dressing table. She sat down on the stool before it and looked at herself in the mirror. In the reflection she could see Genevieve, still watching her. She looked down at the table and picked up the heavy gilded hairbrush, running it through her long black locks.

'What have you been doing today?' she asked Genevieve's reflection.

'I made a new friend,' Genevieve told her. 'Someone you used to know.'

'Oh?' Elise said, arching her eyebrow.

'Yes, Emelie,' Genevieve continued. 'You remember Emelie, of course. A very pretty girl, blonde and graceful. She worked here once.'

'Oh, yes,' Elise muttered. 'And where did you meet her?'

'She lives a few miles from here.' Elise turned on the stool to face her friend, interested in what she was hearing. 'It was once her husband's home, apparently, but he's left her.'

'Oh,' Elise said, looking quizzical. 'You wouldn't, by any chance, mean the old hunting lodge, would you?'

'I don't know.'

'We own a hunting lodge in the woods. Because it was so seldom used an old employee of ours, Pierre Narbonne, asked my father a few years ago if he could live there. My father agreed, and then probably forgot about it. Emelie must have married Pierre. So that's what happened to her... But the old lodge is de Tranville property.'

'She's a lovely girl,' Genevieve muttered.

'I know,' Elise acknowledged, and then fell silent, and staring at Genevieve, she continued brushing her hair. Genevieve watched her thoughtfully, and Elise felt her quiet gaze, quirkily lowering the hairbrush to her thighs and passing it lightly over the dark curls between her thighs. Genevieve's face reddened.

'It was a shame how our little lesson was so rudely interrupted the other night,' Elise mused. 'We were only just starting and we haven't yet managed to finish.'

'I thought your stepfather had finished it.'

'Well not as far as I'm concerned. So come over here.'

'But what if he finds us?' Genevieve asked anxiously.

'He won't, he's in town. Now, we were learning about submission. Come here.'

Genevieve obediently lifted the sheet and slipped out of bed, stepping lightly to Elise.

'Not like that,' Elise snapped playfully. 'Get down on your hands and knees and crawl to me. Crawl like a cur.'

Genevieve paused. 'Must I?' she whispered.

'Yes, you must, now do as I say and crawl,' Elise commanded.

Genevieve obeyed again, and looked up to find Elise had parted her thighs, beckoning Genevieve towards their lush centre, lewdly massaging her succulent sex lips. 'You remember my little pleasure bud?' Elise whispered. 'Now finish kissing it for me...'

Genevieve swallowed and moved her mouth to Elise's crotch, passing her tongue over it nervously. It was warm and wet. She closed her eyes and let her tongue flicker, gently passing it over the spot she had kissed before. Then Elise's hand roughly clasped the back of her head again, pulling it tighter into the fragrant warmth.

'That's it, slave,' Elise sighed, her buttocks squirming on the stool. She looked down over Genevieve's lovely blonde head, bobbing quietly between her thighs.

Bending forward she ran her hands over Genevieve's back, stroking her from buttocks to shoulders.

Then, on a whim, she looked at the hairbrush in her hand, and Genevieve's buttocks seemed so unsuspecting, quivering away prettily as she licked. Laughing to herself quietly, Elise massaged the back of Genevieve's head with one hand and then brought the brush down with a thwack on the side of Genevieve's bottom, a shocked gasp instantly bursting from the kneeling girl.

She pulled back and stared at Elise blankly, the pain intense and unexpected, destroying the passionate concentration into which she had drifted. What was the enigmatic girl doing to her? Why had she done that? She crawled to her so obediently, kissed her so intimately, so why hit her?

Getting to her feet Emelie suddenly flashed into Genevieve's mind, and the words of the pretty girl came back. The warning...

With tears in her eyes she'd told her of how Elise had played games with her heart. And what was happening to her now? She was being taught how to enjoy, but to enjoy what? The cruel whims of Elise...

'Come back here, silly,' Elise ordered, but Genevieve shook her head, and turning rebelliously she grabbed her discarded nightdress and slippers from the foot of her bed and ran out of the room, along the landing and down the stairs.

In a panic she stood in the hall, not knowing what to do. She wanted to get away but where would she go? Hastily putting on her nightdress and slippers she caught sight of the old woollen cloak Emelie had lent her. She hurried to it and threw it around her shoulders, again fastening it at her throat.

Emelie, she had been so sweet and kind. She would go to her now, the only person she could turn to. Genevieve raced to the front door, unlocked it hurriedly and ran out into the cold night.

After disciplining Elise and Genevieve in his library, Count de Tranville passed a restless night.

The desirability of the two girls had been so deeply embedded in his mind, and as he tried to sleep taunting images of them, submissive and beautiful, swirled in his head and left him with an erection he was forced to relieve by his own hand.

He knew in his heart that the whole event was of Elise's doing, yet he had punished poor Genevieve more severely than her. He knew he was doing it, and he had enjoyed punishing them both so much that he was within a hairsbreadth of fucking one or both of them.

Genevieve had surprised him, clearly getting lustful as her punishment was administered. He remembered how deliciously she writhed on the desktop, causing his cock to strain against the confines of his clothing.

The next day he went into town to finalise affairs before his departure. Rodolfo would be arriving the following week and then they would begin their journey to the port of La Rochelle, and then by boat to Portugal... and then what?

He arrived in Rency early in the morning and went to the bank immediately to withdraw his gold.

Placing it within secret compartments under the bench of his coach he then went to see two acquaintances whom he knew to be loyal to the old regime, and who might be able to see that his estate would remain untouched and held safely until his eventual return from abroad - for return he surely would when the madness sweeping France was finally over. They were the notaries Michel Germaine-Troyes and Achille de Bourgogne, two respected gentlemen used to dealing exclusively with the affairs of the nobility. The two proved extremely sympathetic to the count's plight, and assured him that they would do their best to legally safeguard his home and possessions.

At around midday he finished with them, and as they wished him farewell and good luck he wondered what to do for the rest of the day. But he felt no urgency to return home.

He instructed his coachman, a loyal old servant who had been with the family for many years, to return to the chateau and unload the gold into the safety of the cellars, then to return to Rency in the evening and meet him in a small inn at the town's entrance.

Alone, the count walked through the streets considering how this would be the last time he saw the place for several years. He stopped at the square, where groups of merchants stood selling their wares before the town hall. Fruit sellers, fishmongers, cobblers, many were there to make some money out of something. Bright colours and twittering sounds came from one stall on a corner of the square, and he approached it.

An old man was selling colourful caged birds, and the count gazed at the beautiful exotic creatures. They were canaries, parrots and minor birds; birds from the New World, and they talked! Birds that repeated names. 'Robespierre!' exclaimed one. 'Marat!' squawked another.

Perhaps it might be nice to buy a few and take them home to impress Elise and Genevieve, he considered. But they would be leaving very soon, he reflected, and it would be silly to start burdening their journey with extra baggage.

After a while he found a tavern, and by early afternoon he had lunched and, growing melancholy, gone through three bottles of red wine.

A little later he found another tavern, and talking intermittently with passing locals, he managed to drink three mugs of beer, another bottle of wine and two glasses of a local brandy.

As the late afternoon drew on, the count, slightly tipsy to say the least, made his way to another tavern that turned out to also be the local brothel. He sat, and was soon approached by two of the hostelry's wenches. Both were plain and well-used things, but the count was bored and pleased to talk with them. They were keen to take him to a room, but he gazed at them wearily. One was blondish, short and chubby and missing a front tooth. The other was darker, round-faced and heavy-hipped. The count saw nothing to excite him.

But, as his mind kept going back to his two charges and as he drank even more, he decided to go along with the two whores, so he went to their room.

He didn't ask them to undress. Instead he told them both to bend over and lift their skirts, and as the two, side by side, squatted with their flabby bare bottoms in the air, he skewered them both, absentmindedly passing his member from one to the other, slapping and groping their fat buttocks.

He moved from one to the other, humping one for a few minutes, then humping the other for a few minutes, before finally telling them he'd had enough. He didn't find the steam to ejaculate into either of them, but he paid them both well.

By the early evening Count de Tranville was just about sober enough to remember his rendezvous with his coach at the arranged inn. He staggered through the darkening streets, but no coach was to be seen at the front of the designated hostelry, so he decided to go in and carry on drinking until it arrived.

About half an hour later the coachman arrived to find his employer in a snoring, drunken sleep inside, slumped across an ale-soaked table. He had drunk more than six bottles of wine, four mugs of beer and four brandies by that time.

The driver carried him to the coach, and de Tranville slumped in one corner as they rattled homeward, gazing with bloodshot, uncomprehending eyes at the passing countryside. His head began reeling with thoughts of the females that were beginning to complicate his life.

Madame Coubette... she was still attractive, but with the nagging and the jealousies it was clear that she was becoming a problem. It would have to end, but how to do it without too much bitterness?

How tempting Elise was, he considered. She was truly a delicious feast. Her eyes came back to him. He could see them staring, smouldering beneath the fringe of dark hair. They had weighed him up. They thanked him for the punishment delivered, and then asked for more. They saw the craving inside him, the craving he fought to suppress in the name of decency, the craving that manifested itself and was noted by her as a significant bulge in his breeches. How her sultry eyes had gazed at this shameful evidence, her moist lips pouting, silently beckoning him...

If she were to stay with him alone it would be too tempting, he knew. No, something would have to be arranged. He would have to engineer a suitable marriage for her, to remove her as a temptation. But who would be suitable, during such volatile times?

Then his befuddled thoughts weaved their way to Genevieve. How precious a beauty she was, too! Growing lustful he recalled her timid nakedness, so unaware of the exquisiteness of her innocence and loveliness. He remembered her as she undressed, and how hard it had been to resist latching his lips to those rosy nipples on perfect breasts as she coyly loosened her camisole. How fine were those buttocks that quivered before him as he rained his crop down upon them. He had sought to meet her eyes after the beating but she looked at him too fleetingly, shame and pain covering her face and making her eyes tearful. And yet during the beating he had distinctly seen how her hips squirmed. Oh yes, she was so coy, but there was a female of passion beneath.

Strange, though, he considered; he had punished her more than Elise, fully knowing she was almost certainly innocent of any wrong. Could he, perhaps, have stronger feelings for her than he'd ever realised? It must be so...

And it was as he reflected on the lovely Genevieve that the thought suddenly struck him; a marriage between a de Tranville and a de Montvert would be a very fine match! Why had it never occurred to him before? Yes, it was not a bad idea at all.

He was getting on in years, he knew, and for so long now, it seemed, he had been in mourning. His home had become a shrine to the dark sorceress that was Elise's mother. Surely this could not go on forever? Surely, sooner or later, it would be time to pull back the veil of darkness and let the light of summer break into his life again. And the fair girl, why she was as close to the wonder of a bright new day as any girl could be. Yes, the idea was a splendid one!

As the plan took root in the count's tipsy head he began to grow cheerful. Things might not be so bad after all, with a new and beautiful wife. They would still have to go to Portugal as exiles it was true, but surely not forever. And one day he would return, his treasure of a young wife by his side, and then, perhaps, they would have heirs.

He would have to remove Elise from the picture, however. For with her around his cock would never be at peace and could not be trusted to be discreet. Her dark beauty would always shadow him, stirring desires that should be buried. Who could he find as her suitor?

He tried to call to mind the eligible sons of other French nobles he knew. How many were still alive? How many were still in the country? It was impossible to say. But what about the young gentleman who recently dined with them - that dandy, Rodolfo? All right, he was Portuguese. But he was of noble blood. Could a marriage be set between him and Elise? Why not? He would be meeting the young man in a week and soon he would meet his father. Conde de Agora would certainly understand that the wealth and name of the de Tranville's could not be erased by this vicious revolution. The old world order would have to come back sooner or later. So Rodolfo would be marrying into good prospects. They would still have to live in Portugal for some time, but not forever.

The coach drew up at the chateau. The coachman descended to help him again, but the count stepped down unaided. There was even a slight spring in his step. Why hadn't he come up with the marriage ideas before?

What a funny day it had been, he reflected as he entered his home. The morning had been so gloomy, but now he felt good. Perhaps he could tell everyone of his marriage plans now? No, perhaps not, for they would see he was still drunk and not take him seriously. Tomorrow then. But he had cause for celebration now.

The count crossed the hall, sat on the divan in the sitting room and called for a bottle of wine. Elise might moan about her wedding, he pondered, but Rodolfo was a fine young man. Virile too, he didn't wonder, although hopefully not too virile; it wouldn't do if the young stag broke Elise's heart straight away by chasing other girls.

And what of Madame Coubette? He had enjoyed her buxom body and boudoir skills for some long time now. But there was no longer room for her in the picture. She would be hurt, but she was a woman of the world and she would just have to accept life as it was. She was still attractive enough to move on and find someone else with whom to entertain herself.

As the count sipped his wine he soon found himself growing tired, so he stretched out on the divan and fell soundly asleep, a broad, tipsy smile on his face.

Madame Coubette padded around the guest bedroom inquisitively. She had never seen it before, for despite having been to the chateau many times there was so much of the place she hadn't seen.

And how strange, she reflected, that she had formed an alliance with Elise, no less. The girl had always bothered her so much, her mere presence and wilful attitudes always filling her with anger. But now things had changed. Now they actually needed each other.

She had followed her intuition, and cleverly conjured a plan that would solve some of her difficulties. She was sure her decrepit husband was not going to live another winter, and when he died, what would he leave her? He had made promises. He had talked of his will, but each time she alluded to the subject he stubbornly refused to let her see it. She had her own savings, but she would need much, much more to be comfortable in the manner to which she was accustomed.

It was very late and the house was silent, so she decided to leave the room and explore what, if her plans worked out well, would be her home in the near future. With a candle in hand she made her way along the darkened landing outside the bedroom, and from the top of the sweeping staircase she could see the hallway and door of the drawing room below. Why, if the door was left a little open one had a perfect view into the room... ah, so that would explain how the little minx Elise knew about her and the count. It was a very good place for spying, she had to admit.

Madame Coubette went softly down the stairs, and quietly pushed open the first door she came to. It was the library, with book-lined walls and a large portrait hanging above the mantelpiece. Next to the fireplace in the shadows she could make out a leather armchair and a writing desk. The painting piqued her curiosity, and with one hand shielding the candle flame, she approached it.

It was a portrait of a dark-haired woman, a striking beauty. She had large dark eyes and a wide, sensual mouth. Madame Coubette immediately thought of Elise... this was clearly her mother.

Looking away from the portrait, her attention was grabbed by an object lying on the desk. She put the candle down and picked it up. It was a riding-crop made from black leather, with a leather loop at the tip. She swiped it through the air a couple of times, appreciating its threatening whistle. Then she smacked it down on the seat of the armchair. It cracked loudly, the sound exciting her. She smiled - if only she'd had the crop with her earlier; it would have been delicious to feel its cool suppleness scorching the pretty bottom of Genevieve when she had the girl in her grasp. As she picked up the candle again there was a noise from outside the quiet room, so she went to investigate.

There was another muted, snuffling sound coming from the sitting room, so she

45

carefully and quietly opened the door, and saw Count de Tranville sprawled in ungainly fashion on one of the ornate divans, a bottle of wine almost empty on the occasional table beside him, an empty glass on its side on the carpet. He was ruddy-faced and looked exhausted, and as Madame Coubette eyed him he snored loudly, smacked his wet lips together a few times, mumbled something, then started breathing heavily and steadily as his drunken sleep deepened.

Then a plan began to formulate in the crafty woman's head. If she were to keep the count from going to Portugal and commit him to marrying her instead, there wasn't much time to lose. Perhaps the state in which he now wallowed was the key - a glorious opportunity presenting itself.

Carefully she crept back up the stairs, in search of Elise. She tapped lightly on the first few bedroom doors, opening them and whispering the girl's name until she found the correct boudoir. She was asleep, her black hair fanned lustrously on her pillows.

'The count is back,' the woman whispered excitedly, moving into the room and gently shaking the girl's shoulder. 'Are you awake?'

Elise stirred and sat up with a start, naked under the covers. She stretched and yawned, and Madame Coubette smiled at the girl's sleepy beauty.

'Ready?' Elise murmured drowsily. 'Ready for what?'

'Ready for our arrangement,' Madame Coubette said, and Elise stared blankly at her for a moment, struggling to get her muddled thoughts in any sort of order. 'Come on, get up,' Madame Coubette urged in hushed tones. 'Come on, get up, we must act quickly. If you want your desires to be fulfilled come with me now. But remember what we discussed and agreed. I will help you get what you want and in return you must help me.'

Still feeling somewhat confused, Elise allowed the woman to take her hand and ease her out of the comfort of her large bed, the woman eyeing her naked, shapely contours appreciatively.

Elise reached for her discarded nightgown, but the woman stopped her. She looked Elise's voluptuous body up and down, and placed the candle on the dresser. Gently she touched Elise's breasts and stroked her nipples, smiling as she felt them harden responsively.

'What red-blooded male could say no to you, my dear?' she whispered huskily, moistening her lips. 'Such beauty should not be covered, it should be flaunted.' With her eyes still on Elise, Madame Coubette picked up the candle again and took her hand.

'What are you doing?' Elise asked.

'I'm showing you how to get what you want,' the woman told her. 'Sometimes directness is the only way. Trust me.'

Guiding the naked beauty out of the room and along the shadowy landing, Madame Coubette paused as she reached the staircase. It was the spot overlooking the drawing room.

'It's here that you watched us, isn't it?' she said, and Elise nodded honestly. 'Well, your time has now come. Go to him. He's down in the sitting room.' She patted Elise softly on the bottom, encouraging her to move, and together they crept down the stairs, the woman a few steps behind.

As they crossed the wide hall and slipped into the sitting room, Madame Coubette pulled Elise closer to her. 'You must kiss him,' she instructed in hushed tones. 'Kiss him the way you've seen me kiss him. Kiss him as if you were licking honey from a spoon...'

Elise's heart was racing. Was this really happening? Was it possible that she would...?

'Go on, he's asleep...' the woman urged. 'Kiss him while he slumbers and doesn't know whether he's dreaming, awake, or drunk.'

Still feeling drowsy herself, and with her head in a spin from the speed of the unexpected events, Elise lowered herself to her knees.

'Go on...' Madame Coubette whispered again.

Elise gazed at the count uncertainly. She was naked and kneeling right between his splayed legs. She froze, unable to continue.

A light smack resounded against her bottom. 'Suck him!' Madame Coubette hissed. 'Remember your part of the bargain! Don't let me down now!'

Elise wasn't sure that she'd actually entered into any bargain, but she brushed back her hair and squeezed even closer to the sleeping count, her heart thudding. There he was, the man who had always seemed so unobtainable. She moved her face closer, watching his heavy chest slowly rising and falling as he breathed.

A second smack fell lightly across her buttocks, and she let the warm smarting sensation seep through her. It felt undeniably good. How humbled she was before her stepfather, and the thought made her pussy pulse. She gazed up at his rugged features, and then at the clearly evident swelling lifting the crotch of his breeches. What - or who - was he dreaming about?

Her hands tingled. There were five buttons straining to keep his breeches decently fastened. She fumbled nervously with the first; terrified by the body breathing heavily before her, terrified he might wake at any moment and be furious and disgusted by what she was doing.

The second and third buttons opened more easily, but as she undid the fourth his snores stopped abruptly in his nasal passages. Elise froze until his breathing resumed, more quietly than before, the heat from his loins radiating through his breeches to her motionless hands, which could do nothing but rest anxiously on the lump still hidden within his partially opened clothing.

She unfastened the last button and watched as the breeches parted and revealed nothing to her eyes but tormenting shadows. His clothing still highlighted the prominence of his semi-hard manhood, but loyally refused to disclose it to her wide-eyed searching.

'Don't worry,' the woman encouraged in an eager whisper, 'he's so drunk that if he rouses he'll think he's dreaming. But unlike most, this will be a dream he'll never forget. Now suck him.'

Elise took a deep breath, and then slipped her hand into the beckoning shadows wherein his penis lurked. Her fingertips located it immediately, and it was warm to the touch. It pulsed as though alive, and summoning her courage she took it in her hand. She tugged it out gently, her fingers timorously sensing its warm pulse as it stood tall and proud before her spellbound face. Its purplish head shone before her lips with the same arrogance it had shown to Madame Coubette. Elise's heart beat furiously, and for a moment she felt like fleeing.

'Go on,' Madame Coubette whispered, raising her hand as if to smack the kneeling girl again, but instead she slowly lowered it and traced the girl's soft buttocks, running her fingertips between the cheeks and over her dark bottom hole, then even lower to her damp pussy lips. Elise shuddered and gasped at the intimate touch.

'Suck him,' Madame Coubette directed again, and Elise obediently closed her eyes and then covered the head of her stepfather's erection with her lips.

'That's it!' Madame Coubette whispered. 'Like licking honey off a spoon...'

Elise sucked, her cheeks hollowing as she gazed up at the sleeping count. She let his member plop from her mouth and moved her tongue to its tip. Then, as she had done to Rodolfo, she teased it with a few lingering licks. She nibbled it gently then swallowed it again, tightened her lips around it and gently started bobbing her head up and down.

A smack from the woman's hand impacted on her bottom, rocking her forward slightly and making her clamp her mouth harder over the count's standing stem, feeling its ridges rubbing her tongue, his helmet pushing out against one cheek and then the other. The column of living flesh was expanding, filling her mouth. Her pussy radiated heat. It was soaking wet.

With a dip of her head she felt the count's penis nudging the back of her throat, making her lose her breath and shudder. A rasping, alcohol-laden sigh wafted from his slack lips. His snoring had stopped but he was still breathing heavily, and keen to conclude the task, Elise tightened her lips around him even more and sucked harder.

'Mmm, Elise...' he murmured, and she froze, her mouth still clamped to his cock, her wide eyes watching him for any signs of waking. But he was still comatose, mumbling her name in his sleep. 'Elise,' he mumbled again. 'Elise, take your clothes off for me...' He was dreaming of her, and he was undressing her in his sleep!

She licked the salty heat of his member, and it seemed to grow hotter with each flick of her tongue. It was large, though perhaps not as large as Rodolfo's. She let her fingers pull back the ridge of skin below the helmet, watching how it expanded. She took hold of his balls, weighing them in her palm.

Moving her mouth to him again, she ran her tongue from the base of her stepfather's cock to its bulbous tip, and smoothed her lips over it again, then squealed softly as the indecent fingers between her thighs located and teased her clitoris.

'Now stand up,' the woman instructed, and Elise did as bidden, allowing the woman to turn her. She was stunned as Madame Coubette kissed her, unable to resist the unexpected invasion, the woman's tongue worming into her mouth. An uninvited hand slid between her thighs, and another cupped her breast, and despite her shock and confusion the girl was so turned on!

Madame Coubette lowered herself and knelt beside the count, stroking his standing cock familiarly. 'Come... sit down,' she whispered to Elise. 'Straddle him and lower yourself onto this magnificent specimen of manhood. I'll guide you.'

Still utterly dumbfounded by the enormity and unexpectedness of what was happening, Elise nodded, and then turning her back to the kneeling woman and the count, she eased back over his thighs. She paused, wondering if this was proper, then felt Madame Coubette's hand on her bottom. Then with a start she felt the bloated helmet of the count prising her pussy lips open. She sighed and shuddered, unsure about the wisdom of all this, and then she gasped and held her breath as the stout stalk pierced her virginal channel.

'Your first time?' Madame Coubette gloated. 'Well, I would never have guessed.'

Elise squirmed, instinctively wriggling her hips and bottom to ease the strange discomfort, feeling like a piece of meat on a skewer.

Suddenly the count stirred fully and bellowed his alarm, shoving her fiercely in the back, thrusting her off his lap and sending her sprawling onto the floor.

He was instantly fully awake, gawping down at her in horror. His mouth opened and shut a few times as he searched for the words with which to express his utter astonishment, and then he jumped up from the divan, his breeches slipping down to his knees. His disbelieving eyes flickered from his cringing stepdaughter to the kneeling Madame Coubette. For a moment his cock was still humiliatingly swollen, bobbing stiffly before him from beneath his shirttails.

'What... what on earth is going on here?' he eventually bellowed, but while he glared down at her, Elise took the decision that having started she could not make matters worse if she brought the task to a conclusion. She had no idea why she thought that to be the best course of action in the circumstances, but think it she did. And so she got back up on her knees before him, and as he watched in unreserved amazement, she took his cock in her fist and fed it back into her own mouth. He didn't shove her away again, so deciding that he was too dumbfounded to object any further, she sucked avidly, as if refusing to be separated from it again.

And he was too stunned to speak or reject her attentions again. Instead his hands fell to the back of her gently bobbing head and his fingers clamped in her silky black hair as he instinctively guided her movements, wet suckling sounds filling the still room. In the face of such exquisite torment his crisis was approaching fast, so he clutched her head even tighter, pulling her face to his groin until he felt her cute nose and stretched lips nuzzling his pubic hair, and fight it though he tried, he couldn't help but grind his hips forward, pushing himself deeper into the warmth of her clutching throat.

Madame Coubette stared at them in awe, a faint smile gradually playing about her features. She'd had no idea how well her little plan would develop.

The count's hips began to move more raggedly as he fucked Elise's mouth, his talon-like fingers moving her head back and forth at an increasing pace, and then he grunted wildly as he came, filling her sweet mouth with his seed, his pale buttocks hollowing in unison with each eruption.

Madame Coubette, absolutely entranced by the eroticism of the scene before her, wrapped her arms around Elise's shoulders and the count's thighs and hugged them both, squeezing the kneeling girl even closer to the standing man as the girl desperately swallowed his copious seed.

Genevieve clutched the cloak tightly around her shoulders as she ran and staggered through the dark night, her only light provided by the silvery crescent moon. She could feel the harsh chill of the wind tugging the material as she clutched it tightly about her. She shivered and breathed heavily as the rising wind buffeted about her. Her heart pounded as she thought desperately of the small lodge and the security and comforts her new friend Emelie would offer, the wind seeming to unite with the darkness and the angry forest to frighten her. The night was mocking her plight, laughing at her, telling her what a silly thing she was and that she should return to the chateau.

She ran for what seemed an endless time, and each time she did stop to catch her breath some noise from the forest would startle her again, and she would once more dash onward.

It began to rain lightly, the wind was still biting, and as she ran she could feel the cloak being snatched and tugged by angry gusts and gnarled branches and undergrowth.

How far could it be now? Was she lost? How long had she been fleeing the chateau? A cool sweat beaded her skin and her chest was pounding painfully, filled by the chilly night air. The drizzly rain had dampened the cloak, making it heavy and cold.

Eventually, and to her great relief, she saw the dark outline of the small lodge silhouetted a short distance ahead. She slowed her pace, feeling her heart slowing too, and her panting eased. Then a burst of thunder suddenly roared overhead and the rain turned from a misty drizzle to a downpour.

Quickly she approached, and could now see the light escaping from the cracks in the closed shutters and beneath the front door.

Wearily, she pounded the latter, waited some moments then raised her hand to try again, but as she did so it creaked open very slightly.

'Miss Genevieve!' Emelie gasped. 'Why, what an earth has happened to you?'

Genevieve stared forlornly into the warm blue eyes of the lovely blonde girl, her heart filling with gratitude at the genuine concern etched on the girl's face.

'Emelie...' she gasped desperately, 'can I stay with you? I need your help...'

With Madame Coubette's arm wrapped firmly around her shoulders, and her stepfather's wilting but still pulsing penis in her mouth, the enormity of what Elise had just done began to sink in.

The taste of his seed filled her mouth, its saltiness lingering on her tongue. She moved her flushed face back a little and allowed his penis to flop from between her lips, the last of his sticky emission coating them. Then guiltily she peeped up at him, and his expression and demeanour chilled her.

'What loathsome debauchery have you two whores plotted?' he roared, aggressively shrugging both females disdainfully away. Elise cowered and looked up at him, his cock still dangling limply before her, an elongated drip of semen hanging from its shrinking head.

Noticing the direction of her gaze, the count quickly hoisted and refastened his breeches. His accusatory glare then switched from the naked beauty before him to the older woman to his side. 'You planned to catch me thus,' he snarled coldly, a look of loathing distorting his face. 'You harpies connived to catch me at my weakest moment, to carry out this grotesque betrayal.' He swooned a little, his head still pounding from the effects of the day's heavy drinking. What on earth had Elise done? It was monstrous... but how sweet her lips had felt, suckling on his cock... they still glistened with the evidence of just how much he had relished her efforts... and as for that wicked little tongue of hers...

Exhausted and confused he slumped back onto the divan. 'Get out of my sight, now,' he said wearily, rubbing his tired, bloodshot eyes. 'Or I'll beat the life out of you both.'

Elise rose slowly, standing proud and voluptuous before him, her eyes gazing into his, her glistening lips slightly parted, her tongue passing slowly over them as she searched his expression for some trace of compassion or forgiveness. But there was no pardon to be found there, and she felt herself sob deeply within. How could he turn on her so? It wasn't her idea. She lowered her eyes remorsefully, and began to turn.

'Let us not continue this hypocrisy any longer,' Madame Coubette said, interrupting the tense silence. 'Elise, stay where you are.

'Why, look at her, you fool,' she went on scornfully to the count. 'Isn't she the most gorgeous thing you've ever seen?'

Elise raised her head and stared boldly at her stepfather, her ripe breasts swaying gently as she shifted anxiously on her feet, and the count absorbed her shapely contours with barely concealed avarice.

'You know she is,' Madame Coubette continued. 'And she is here, before you, begging you to take her as and when you please. All she wants is to share in your passion, for you to stop pretending you don't desire her?'

'Silence!' the count snapped. 'What you are saying is insane, woman. Utterly insane. Why, she's...'

'She's not your daughter, you fool.' It was Madame Coubette's turn to interrupt. 'She's a beautiful young woman who lives with you and who offers herself for your pleasure, and who will share you with your wife.'

'What the hell are you talking about?' he demanded. 'I have no wife, you stupid?!'

'Your plan to go away to Portugal is one of pure folly,' she interrupted again, unperturbed by his anger. 'Think it through. You know that if you go you will lose your property and holdings here forever, and there will be no turning back. You will lead a life of emptiness and exile, dependent on the charity of foreigners.'

Madame Coubette smiled conspiratorially at Elise, and even had the temerity to cast her a surreptitious wink, unseen by the count. 'But, if you were to marry me,' she went on, looking confidently back at the man slouched on the divan, 'it would be acknowledged that you are not a supporter of the nobility, and you would not be seen as being of any threat or concern to the revolution.'

He frowned, his aching head churning over her words.

'You would keep your home, and land, and money,' the woman went on relentlessly. 'You would have me as your bed-mate and useful wife, and you would have her, this beautiful girl, who you secretly yearn for.'

He looked at her without speaking, his brow furrowing as he reflected on the woman's words. She turned to Elise.

'Look at her,' Madame Coubette told him, passing a hand over one of the girl's rosy cheeks. 'I am your security in France, and this girl is your willing, hidden treasure.'

De Tranville looked at Elise's beauty thoughtfully for several moments, and then at the woman. 'Do you honestly think that a person of my standing could, in his right mind, marry a woman known to be a whore and an adulteress?' he said viciously, his eyes cold. 'What foolishness has taken hold of your brain to dream up such things? Elise is very beautiful, as was her mother. And she has always been wild of temperament, I know that. But it has been an honour for me to try and raise her in a way that would meet her mother's approval, and to consider anything beyond that is utterly inconceivable.'

Madame Coubette frowned, sensing herself losing the initiative.

'I have done much thinking today and I have reached a decision over the future which may hurt you, but which is inevitable,' he continued. 'Madame, our relationship is over. The fact that you are entertaining ideas of marriage only proves to me that my kindness toward you has not only made you forget your station, but has pushed you to near lunacy. You are already married, and do not forget that fact.

'As for you, Elise, it is time for you to marry, too.'

'Me, marry?' Elise blurted. 'Marry who?'

'The suitor I have in mind is Rodolfo de Agora,' he told her matter-of-factly. 'He is a perfect match for you, given our circumstances. We will go to Portugal and you will marry him, or another man of his standing... he has three brothers. I, meanwhile, also have a mind to marry, but I am planning to marry Genevieve de Montvert.'

'You are *what?*' Madame Coubette shrieked.

'I was a close friend of her father, and ultimately, we're of the same stock. It seems like a logical move.'

Both Elise and Madame Coubette were stunned by the shock of his plan. A mere slip of a girl was taking away the man for whom the two of them vied. She had trumped them and they stared dumbly at the count, who now bore a triumphant smirk.

'If, however, you do not wish to marry Rodolfo,' he went on to Elise, 'there are plenty of convents in Lisbon. Either way, it is clear that it is time for you to learn to fend for yourself.'

'And what of me?' Madame Coubette demanded shrilly.

'What of you?' he echoed. 'That is the business of your husband.'

Madame Coubette's mighty bosom began to heave with her indignation. The woman started sobbing, her bold face crumpled.

'And now,' he announced, somewhat pleased with himself, 'it is late. We will talk further tomorrow. Now the both of you will get upstairs to your beds.'

The deflated pair turned, but Madame Coubette paused for a moment and then turned back, her eyes narrowed. 'If you stick to this plan you will never leave France alive,' she vowed vehemently.

'I want you gone by the morning,' the count responded indifferently. 'And thereafter I do not want to see you again.'

Madame Coubette was beaten, but Elise had recovered her spirit, her eyes shining darkly. 'Of all the women you could marry, Genevieve would be the worst choice,' she started. 'Have you forgotten how you recently found her with me? Do you not remember why you beat her?'

'I did beat her,' he acknowledged. 'But it was a miscarriage of justice, I have little doubt. It was more than likely that her behaviour was engineered and inspired by you.'

'That is where you couldn't be more mistaken,' Elise insisted. 'Genevieve is unable to love men. She told me so. It was for that reason that you found her as you did, with me. I felt pity for her, and I let her take some pleasure?'

'You lie,' he interrupted.

'It was the same with that pretty maid, remember? Emelie? She too had confessed that she knew only how to love women, and that's why you found us as you did. You have mistaken my compassion for depravity.'

'Do you really expect me to believe that?' he challenged.

'You should, for I believe Genevieve and Emelie have become friends. Why, only today Genevieve went to visit her, and she has still not returned. You can check her bedroom, if you so wish.'

'What are you talking about?' he said, but without conviction. 'Emelie the kitchen maid was sent away from here two years ago.'

'That's right,' Elise agreed. 'But she lives in the old hunting lodge you lent to Jacques. The two of them have been meeting in secret, to enjoy their sexual pleasures,

pleasures for which you have branded me as depraved. Why, Genevieve is the depraved one, yet you plan to marry her.'

'This cannot be true!' the count exclaimed.

'So depraved, in fact,' Elise continued unremittingly, 'that she even made her passions known to Madame Coubette, who being your loyal mistress, naturally rejected them.'

A cunning smile simmered in Madame Coubette's eyes. She had nothing but admiration for Elise's wiliness. 'It is true,' she asserted, providing reinforcements to Elise. 'The girl tried to force herself upon me in my very own carriage, taking advantage of my good nature after I had stopped to offer her a ride.'

'If you marry the strumpet, you will be a wretched man,' Elise declared. 'Not only will you be poor and far from home, but you will also be a cuckold and a laughing stock. For I know Genevieve's nature. And not a single pretty lady visitor or slip of a housemaid will escape her lewd attentions.'

Count de Tranville looked at his stepdaughter suspiciously. 'Where is she now?' he asked curtly.

'As I said,' Elise shrugged, 'with her new *friend* in your hunting lodge.'

The man remained pensive and quiet, his head still pounding as his hangover intensified. 'We will see about this tomorrow,' he eventually said without looking at either of them. 'Now go up to your rooms.'


# Chapter Six

Genevieve yawned as she woke up. She had slept through most of what had been a damp morning. It could have been nearly midday when she roused, and for a moment thought she could hear the rumble of an approaching horse and carriage. But the sound soon seemed to fade.

She opened her eyes slowly, and then started; the low rough ceiling above perplexed her at her first. Where was she? She heard a flapping sound and turning her head, saw a chicken strutting beside the small bed upon which she lay. Then she remembered where she was.

She got up and stretched, then wearing only the nightshift Emelie had lent her to sleep in, went to find her new friend.

Emelie was in the tiny kitchen, bent over the sink busily washing some clothes. Genevieve gazed at her quietly. She had tied her blonde hair up in a bun, and a few wisps had escaped and curled elegantly down by her ears.

She was wearing the same simple dress of the previous night, stretched snugly to her bottom, and as she worked her buttocks swayed rhythmically.

Genevieve shook her long hair and passed a hand through it. How dishevelled it must be, she considered, and then tiptoed towards Emelie.

The girl was too lost in her work to hear her approach, but then as Genevieve paused just behind her Emelie realised someone was there and jumped and turned quickly.

'I'm sorry,' Genevieve giggled, 'I didn't mean to startle you.'

Emelie looked at her and laughed too. 'It's all right,' she said brightly.

'What are you doing?' Genevieve asked.

'I'm washing a dress for you,' Emelie replied. 'It's one of mine, but we're the same size and you'll need something to wear other than that nightdress. You can't go about like that forever.'

'Why not?' Genevieve sighed, gazing wistfully into the bright blue eyes of her friend. 'I wish I could, and I wish I could stay here forever.'

'I... I put the cloak to dry over the fire,' Emelie said, somewhat bashfully. 'It'll be ready for you to wear soon, too.'

A sudden feeling of sadness filled Genevieve, for the words only reminded her that she still had plenty to resolve back at the chateau.

'When I woke up this morning I started thinking,' Emelie went on. 'Count de Tranville will surely want to know what's happened to you, so perhaps it's best that you return soon.'

'I know, but I don't want to go back,' Genevieve admitted. 'Can't I stay here with you?'

Emelie passed her hand over Genevieve's cheek, and smiled affectionately. 'No,' she said honestly. 'Life here is not a life for you.'

Tears began to fill Genevieve's eyes. What was she to do now? What was the future to hold for her?

Count de Tranville had not believed Elise and Madame Coubette's tale of Genevieve's alleged depravity. The future had hovered before him too neatly to be so suddenly spoiled by their dubious revelations. But doubt had been sown in his mind, despite him trying to shake it off.

Rodolfo was due to arrive at any day. When he did they would set off together, and in Portugal the marriages would take place. Genevieve would be his young bride, and Rodolfo would be Elise's husband. They would live on the funds he had withdrawn, and the Conde de Agora's hospitality for the year or two it might take for the madness that had swept France to pass. Then he would return to his rightful home.

But the accusations Elise had made about Genevieve unsettled everything. What was left of the night was a restless time for him. He found himself recalling the vision of Genevieve, naked, her bottom curled before him and her innocent face buried between Elise's legs, and he felt himself stirring yet again. And now Elise, his stepdaughter, had performed fellatio on him! It was as unbelievable to consider as it had been to find her kneeling there sucking his cock between her beautiful lips.

In the end he had consented, admittedly, but was it his fault?

Could there be a shred of truth in what Elise told of Genevieve, and Emelie? That it was they, and not her, who had engendered the Sapphic cravenness and debauchery that had possessed Elise?

The more he ruminated, however, the more sleepless he became. His cock throbbed beneath his nightshirt, and for a while he considered going to Madame Coubette to simply relieve the hardness of it. But he had officially ended their relationship.

And what of her proposal? He had rejected it flatly, but though scandalous it was completely logical. Could it be feasible for him? Could he not live quietly and pleasurably in a comfortable *menage a trios* like she had suggested?

For a moment he imagined being with Genevieve, enjoying her each night, and at the same time enjoying Elise's beauty whenever he pleased. How incredible it would be if they could all be together, in the same bed. He reflected how for so long he had watched them both, yearning inside. And now Elise's feelings for him had been declared and half his hidden fancy was now real...

Could he really cast Elise out of his life and into the arms of another man? Was this not the most stupid of stupidities, to reject what he knew he desired more than anything?

But how could he preserve his honour if he gave in to such lewd machinations, the plotting of a whore or procuress?

It was as well for Madame Coubette that he did not seek her out in the early hours, for she, too, had felt restless.

At first she thought of creeping to the count's bedchamber, seeking to seduce him again and win his favours back, but her guile was outweighed by the concern that her actions might too easily arouse his wrath rather than his lust. Perhaps he would throw her out that very night.

And then she thought of Elise and her passions increased, so she crept to the girl's bedchamber to find her broodingly awake and naked beneath the sheets.

Calculatingly she cooed praise for Elise's cunning as well as her beauty, and after coddling the girl with tender words and caresses, she sought out the privacy between the girl's thighs with her mouth.

Elise sleepily allowed her free passage nether-wards, but as the woman kissed and licked she failed to feel herself stirring, until at last she grew impatient and squirmed and panted, imitating passion, immersing her fingers in the red-brown sea of the woman's hair.

After adoring the taste and fragrance of the succulent girl, Madame Coubette rose and told her that, no matter what the future held, she would always remember Elise as an accomplice and sister. But secretly she rejoiced at her victorious conquest of Count de Tranville's stepdaughter.

Elise smiled drowsily and was ready to sleep again, but noting the wide spread of the woman's thighs, the hand that teased the thick bush between them, and the woman's expectant eyes, she realised that the vow of Madame Coubette's friendship was awaiting a seal.

It was as well to clinch their association, she decided, and so with coolly disguised reluctance she drew upon her resolve and returned the homage she'd received, wincing as the animated woman clutched her raven hair and thrust her face between her splayed thighs.

Upon leaving the room Madame Coubette again made her promise of alliance to Elise, who smiled wryly, telling her new collaborator that her promise would be met with equal commitment.

At breakfast the count was distant but courteous to both females, reluctant to look into either's eyes. He informed them curtly that he intended to travel to the old hunting lodge that morning to collect Genevieve, and in light of her tales, he wanted Elise to accompany him.

He then informed Madame Coubette that once he had the girl safely back in his charge, they would travel on together in his coach and see the woman safely home.

The coach ride passed in silence. Elise sat next to de Tranville, and Madame Coubette sat opposite them both, each of them spending the entire journey looking steadfastly out of a window. Nobody uttered a word let alone dare mention the previous night, the atmosphere uncomfortable as each of them brooded.

Eventually they reached the lodge, set back from the rutted road just to the left. They stepped down from the coach and the count instructed the driver to wait for them, then the threesome walked up the path, the only sound the gentle breeze rustling the leaves of the surrounding trees.

It was a grey morning, but although the rain had stopped a fresh downpour threatened.

They reached the front door, but the count noticed that the heavy window shutter to the side hung partly open. He moved closer and pulled it wider, peering in to see a room, a table and chairs, a blazing fire in a stone hearth, and there, standing together in front of the sink, were Genevieve and Emelie.

The count watched, his anger rising as he saw Emelie stroking Genevieve's cheek with an evident affection that could only be proof of what his stepdaughter had told him about the shameful pair. They were talking together, although the lurking man could hear nothing of what they said, and though he would not admit it to himself, they looked happy in each other's company, holding hands with natural ease.

Madame Coubette and Elise peered over the count's shoulders, watching in silent awe, and each without the other knowing it silently celebrating an astonishing piece of good fortune. The fabrications created by Elise about Genevieve and Emelie for the count's benefit were perhaps much closer to the truth than either the scheming stepdaughter or the jilted madame could possibly have hoped. Elise in particular felt utterly vindicated for the allegations she'd made, and actually rather proud of her judgement; the two unwitting girls were fully corroborating the tale she had concocted.

The more Count de Tranville watched the more a rage gripped him, fuelled by the quiet mockery of the two females standing behind him. Elise had told the truth, he had to acknowledge that now. Genevieve was a slattern and a lover of other women, and as such she was unfit to be his wife.

But, he argued with himself, if he abandoned her now to such depraved lusts, would he be guilty of shirking his responsibilities as the girl's guardian? Perhaps he would be doing her a long-lasting and damaging disservice if he were to abandon her to her questionable lusts. Instead of accepting his misjudgement and discarding his plan of marriage, perhaps, for the sake of the girl, he should continue on his previous course of action.

He could still marry Genevieve, he asserted with a silent but fierce determination, he would just have to cleanse her of such dangerously frivolous behaviour. He looked back at the coach and eyed his driver, sitting straight-backed, waiting patiently, respectfully staring ahead at nothing in particular, his short whip gripped in one hand...

A lesson was sorely needed: and it had to be a harsh, lasting lesson.

Count de Tranville made light work of the stout wooden door. He thrust it open and stood framed in the entrance, glaring at the two startled girls.

Emelie shrieked and Genevieve clutched her tight, the girls instinctively using each other for comfort and protection.

He remained silent, staring, his knuckles white he gripped the whip so fiercely. What a despicable spectacle the two girls made to his affronted eyes... but how stunningly beautiful they were.

Like angelic twins. They were the same height, both with the same slim, nubile frame, the same light blonde hair, the same fresh, rosy complexion. Their matching beauty was like something from a fairytale. They were two wood nymphs, caught frolicking by a jealous, angry ogre... but then he shook the fancifully ridiculous thoughts away.

Elise and Madame Coubette blustered in too, the older woman sneering at the speechless girls.

'*Now* do you believe me?' Elise demanded, the smugness in her tone stirring him from the trance in which the vision of the girls had gripped him.

He strode further into the room, the whip held threateningly, then without warning he raised it and slashed it down onto the tabletop beside him, the loud crack making the girls gasp and flinch, hugging each other even more protectively, wondering what they'd done to attract such menace.

Genevieve felt her heart thumping in her chest, staring aghast at Count de Tranville.

'I allowed you to stay in my home because of my deep respect and friendship for your family,' he said to her slowly. 'It was for that reason that I've treated you with affection, as one of my own, but it seems that such generous affection and consideration has been misplaced.'

'She should be severely punished,' Madame Coubette urged. 'And the other little strumpet, too!'

'The first time I found you committing these unnatural practices was with Elise,' he went on, hearing the woman but ignoring her, 'and I punished you in the way I thought best. But even then I punished you with consideration, not sure which of you was the guiltier. It is clear to me now, and I am only sorry that I doubted my dear Elise. Your presence in my home has only brought shame upon me, young lady.'

'But...' Genevieve managed, utterly aghast at the unexpected appearance of Count de Tranville and the two females, and of what he was accusing her, 'we haven't done anything. We're doing nothing wrong. Emelie has been kind enough to?'

'Shame,' he repeated angrily, cutting her off and shifting his stern stare to Emelie, 'such as this girl once brought, too.'

'It's not true!' Emelie blurted defensively.

'You will be silent unless spoken to!' he roared, and she wisely made not another sound. 'What are you doing here anyway?' he demanded. 'I dismissed you and sent you away. What are you doing still on my property?'

'This house was given to me by my husband, Jacques,' Emile told him, lifting her chin defiantly.

The count frowned. 'This lodge was never his to give to anyone,' he told her frankly. 'I let it to him on a peppercorn rent some years ago. Where is he now?'

'He left me,' Emelie confessed.

'I am not surprised,' he said cruelly, widening the smirks on the faces of the two females behind him. 'You are an unnatural little whore who has found her equal in this one,' he nodded at Genevieve, and saw her eyes flicker in the direction of his stepdaughter.

'So, despite all this you still have eyes for my Elise, do you?' he said. 'You depraved little vampire.'

Genevieve fought for something to say, words with which to defend herself against such unjust accusations, but they continued to elude her.

The count stepped back beside the raven-haired girl. 'Tell me,' he went on, still addressing the poor blonde girl, 'when you gaze upon her beauty, what do you feel?'

Genevieve still didn't know what to say.

'Do you feel like a man would feel?' he asked. 'Do you feel you want to kiss her and touch her like a man would?'

Genevieve stared at Elise, her cheeks burning, but still she failed to defend herself, and as she faltered he moved with surprising speed and agility, grabbed her wrist and flung her facedown across the table. She shrieked, but it was too late to take evasive action, and before she knew what was happening a large hand between her shoulders pinned her down and his other raised, the whip held aloft.

'Now, you little hussy, let's see if you will learn *this* lesson!' he hissed, his eyes wild with rage. 'So tell me, what are you feeling now?' he provoked through gritted teeth. 'Do you feel lusty still? Would you like to make improper with my stepdaughter again?'

Without giving the restrained girl a chance to respond he swung his arm powerfully down, cracking the whip across her unprotected bottom. Thankfully the nightdress offered a little protection, though it was scant and the cruel strike still caused Genevieve immense hurt.

'What you feel is only natural for someone with a cock!' he taunted. 'So you must learn that unnatural desires only bring pain and shame. And it is pain and shame you will remember every time you look at another of your own gender, you reprehensible creature!'

'Please,' Genevieve managed at last, 'please, sir, I do not deserve this!'

'You will be quiet and accept your punishment with dignity!' he roared, and then as the other three females looked on - two with wicked triumph sparkling in their eyes, the third rooted to the spot in shock at what was unravelling before her - his arm powered down again and the whip cracked viciously against the bent girl's hindquarters, the awesome sound muffled only very slightly by the cotton of her nightdress.

Beneath his hand the count felt sweet Genevieve's back stiffen and her lithe frame attempt to arch up rebelliously against his hold, and it amazed him how the actuality of restraining her on the tabletop, and the spirit indicated by her attempted resistance, transmitted extremely pleasurable sensations to his groin, and he realised his cock was stiffening significantly inside his breeches. He gazed down at her pert buttocks, tormented by the thin white cotton that hid them from his hungry stare.

Fear filled Genevieve. The eyes of everyone were upon her. Her shame was so great she felt light-headed, sure she was about to faint at any moment.

Behind her stepfather Elise lurked, like a voluptuous princess of some dark and savage kingdom, relishing the display before her and congratulating herself for such a successful outcome - better than she could ever have hoped for when the seeds of a plan began to propagate the night before. Her breasts quivered faintly with her breathing, for there was something darkly erotic about what was happening to naïve little Genevieve. Her stepfather raised his arm again and she held her breath, feeling her nipples tingle deliciously.

The whip swept down again and Genevieve wailed, tears trickling down her cheeks and wetting the scrubbed tabletop. Her eyes were tightly closed against the pain and shame. The bite of the whip stung increasingly.

*Svit!* It cut down across her buttocks again, causing her to sob aloud and the three onlookers to gasp - two in admiration for the count, one in sympathy for Genevieve. The pain of the beating was spreading from its various points of contact and making her whole bottom alive with heat... but she could feel the treacherous heat between her thighs shamefully merging with the heat in her buttocks.

Then the count grunted his frustration at the protecting shift, slammed the whip on the table and hoisted the interfering garment up to her waist. Then, without pausing, he delivered a fusillade of smacks to her naked bottom and thighs with the flat of his palm. Genevieve wailed and put her hands protectively back to her punished bottom, but he ordered her to lay her arms on the table above her head and to stop complaining, then for the next few minutes the only sounds in the small lodge was flesh striking flesh and the distraught girl's pleas for mercy. He became a man possessed, his bulging eyes devouring the way her mouth-wateringly curvaceous buttocks quivered beneath each noisy impact, the unexpected and secret pleasure he experienced in spanking her almost making him forget why he was dispensing the punishment in the first place.

Eventually his arm slowed and the chastisement came to an end, Genevieve lying exhausted on the scrubbed pine and the count breathing heavily, his shoulders slumped, his palm tingling pleasantly. He gazed down at her beaten, blotchy buttocks, and for the first time in his life he experienced a powerful yet inexcusable urge to expose his erection and feed it between those deliciously firm globes, pierce her tight anus and relieve himself deep in her most private passage. From where had such an unnatural desire surfaced?

'Now,' he said to Genevieve, quickly pulling himself together and suppressing the aberrant thought, 'whenever you are tempted by unnatural urges, you will know and remember what pain and shame they bring. Do you understand me?' Still slumped over the table she nodded, sobbing more quietly now. 'You will thank me one day for ridding you of such deviant weakness.

'And you,' he said, turning to Emelie, 'will get off my property this instant, before I lose my good humour and have you arrested as a trespasser.'

Emelie burst into tears. 'But, what will I do? Where will I go?'

The count gazed at her blankly. 'That is not my concern,' he said, then turned and walked out of the lodge.

Count de Tranville's anger had faded by the time they reached the chateau. In the capacious hall he put his arm around Genevieve's shoulder, and she looked up at him with timid surprise. Gently he put his finger under her chin, smiled, and then told her to go upstairs, bathe and rest. He wanted to speak to her privately that evening.

He turned to Elise, and felt acutely uncomfortable with how she again made him feel, for the sheer danger her beauty and poise represented for him made his penis thicken in his breeches. He quickly dismissed the treacherous thoughts entering his head and told her to assist her stiffly moving friend. For a moment she stared at him silently, rebelliously, but then nodded and aided the blonde girl upstairs.

Having savoured a hot bath Genevieve put on a freshly laundered nightdress, wincing as the delicate white cotton kissed her beaten bottom, and sat very carefully on the stool in front of her dressing table mirror. She felt warm and refreshed, but her buttocks were still smarting.

She gazed at her reflection, and thought of Emelie. What would happen to her now? She had been thrown out of her home, so what was to become of her?

It was all Genevieve's fault. She closed her eyes and remembered the girl's face and her tender nature. Tears welled in her eyes, just as Elise entered brusquely without knocking.

She picked up a brush and began stroking it through Genevieve's silky blonde hair. 'Why did you run away last night?' she asked.

'You frightened me,' Genevieve told her frankly.

'It was a prank. A sexy little game.'

'I didn't find it so.' Genevieve looked into Elise's eyes in the mirror. 'It hurt me.'

Elise put the brush down on the dressing table, her expression enigmatic. 'Don't tell me you didn't like it,' she said. 'You can't hide your feelings from me. Do you think I couldn't tell?'

Elise squeezed her shoulders and gently began massaging them. Genevieve let her head sink, and gazed down at her hands in her lap. She wanted to be angry with Elise, but she still adored her friend too much, despite everything.

'Do you know who's arriving tomorrow?' Elise asked matter-of-factly.

'No, who?'

'Rodolfo,' Elise announced, searching the young blonde's eyes for a reaction. Genevieve fell silent, a slight blush shading her cheeks. 'And do you know what the count wants to talk to you about this evening?' Genevieve shook her head. 'He's going to ask for your hand in marriage.' Elise's beautiful eyes glowed mischievously.

'I beg your pardon?' Genevieve gasped.

'He intends to marry you.'

'Count de Tranville wants to marry me?' Genevieve babbled, her eyes widening in disbelief.

'And he is planning to have your handsome Rodolfo marry me, too.'

'But... but he is so much older than me, and I don't love him.'

'And I don't love Rodolfo,' Elise said tartly. 'So what's that got to do with it?'

'I won't marry him,' Genevieve insisted. 'I don't love him. How could I? How could he even think it, after what he did to me only this morning? And after making poor Emelie homeless, with nowhere to go and no one to help her?'

'That's not important,' Elise interrupted. 'The count always gets his own way.'

'What should I do?'

Elise shrugged. 'Oh, I might have a plan,' she mused.

By late afternoon the count was in his library enjoying a bottle of red wine, contemplating the delicacy of the vintage. Having finished the first bottle within an unwisely short space of time, he called for another.

For a while he sat staring at its lustrous red colour in his glass, lost in thought: that night he would propose to Genevieve!

He would be married again to a beautiful female. But he was tense. His good friend de Montvert would definitely not have approved of the marriage, on the grounds of his daughter's tender years and the consequent age gap between them, but sadly he was dead.

Unfortunately, however, he had created an obstacle to his proposal; after the punishment he'd administered that morning Genevieve would probably be cold towards him. She might well fear him, too.

Perhaps he should have been more diplomatic in the way he dealt with her indiscretions. What could he now do to win back her confidence? How could he make her accept him as a husband and a lover? He pictured her for a moment, how beautiful she was, his cock stirring again, and then he shook the musings from his mind. He had to focus on the situation before him.

The wine was making him drowsy. As he pondered he drank more, and began feeling hungry.

It would soon be time for dinner, during which he would propose to sweet Genevieve...

The sight of Genevieve being whipped and then spanked whilst pinned to the table in the lodge had certainly stirred Madame Coubette's passions - as had the beauty of the lovely girl, Emelie.

And that is why she offered the distraught girl a position of maid at her Rency town house immediately the count banished her from her meagre home. Madame Coubette's anger toward the count had reached its zenith, and as she reached between her parted legs and stroked the silky blonde head of the sexy little morsel she had acquired, she sipped her red wine and reflected upon the steps she had taken to exact revenge on him, a cunning smile lifting the corners of her rouged lips as an inquisitively obedient tongue located her clitoris...

Arriving at the offices of the town's revolutionary committee earlier that afternoon, she had been warmly greeted by her friends there. Then she informed them of a treachery that was afoot - none other than Count de Tranville's collusions with foreign spies and his plan to escape the country. She informed them that a certain Rodolfo de Agora, an aristocrat and a Portuguese spy, had been plotting against the new regime along with de Tranville, and that if they wanted to arrest the two traitors they should pay a visit to Chateau de Tranville much sooner rather than later.

With the accusation and information, and the esteem and trust in which the committee held Monsieur and Madame Coubette, Rodolfo de Agora and Count Guillaume de Tranville were immediately sentenced to be jailed without trial, and guillotined.

Madame Coubette sipped some more wine and then hissed with pleasure as the obediently kneeling girl's tongue compounded her sense of immense satisfaction.

'You can't keep running away from things,' Elise said to Genevieve, who was lying on her bed. The blonde did not want to marry the count and she did not want to go down to dinner.

'But I won't marry him!' she cried, raising herself onto her elbows.

'I know,' Elise said, 'but listen... it's time I told you a little secret.' She moved and sat on the edge of the bed, beside the supine girl. 'I'm in love with my stepfather. And so I don't want you to marry him either.' Genevieve's large blue eyes widened as she absorbed the confession. 'And I know he feels the same about me, too. So tonight I will make love to him, and seal our future together.'

'But, if he loves you...' Genevieve muttered, astounded by what she was hearing, 'why does he want to marry me?'

'He loves us both. He wants us both.'

Genevieve frowned, finding that hard to believe. 'But I don't feel anything for him... at least, not in *that* way.'

'But you do feel something for me,' Elise said confidently. 'In fact, you feel a lot for me, in *that* way, don't you?'

Genevieve gazed at her in silence, and lay motionless as Elise moved slowly and kissed her. Entranced and wickedly excited, she closed her eyes and received the kiss without complaint. She gradually relaxed and opened her mouth, savouring the gentle stroke of Elise's tongue, aware of the dark seductress carefully unfastening the top buttons of her nightdress, but unable or unwilling to resist. A hand wormed inside and cupped her breast, and she breathed deeply. The kiss ended and Genevieve instinctively nibbled the girl's throat.

'I've a plan,' Elise murmured. 'A plan which will force him to marry me instead of you.'

Genevieve's eyes were closed, the bodice of her dress partly open, and Elise was pinching and teasing her nipples through the cotton. They tingled and grew erect at the cool touch, and Genevieve sighed blissfully.

'But I'll need your absolute cooperation,' Elise continued. 'You must trust me.'

Genevieve opened her eyes. 'What do you mean?' she asked dreamily.

Elise sat back, her hand moving again and lying idly inside the cotton slip, feeling the warmth of the blonde girl's flesh. 'We are to go downstairs, and we will show him the nature of what we feel for each other.'

Genevieve's eyes widened. 'Are you mad?' she gasped.

'Trust me,' Elise said, looking deeply at her.

'But...'

Elise put a finger to Genevieve's lips. 'Don't be afraid,' she whispered. 'I will say things to you and about you. I will ask you questions, and you will answer them honestly.' Genevieve's brow furrowed quizzically. 'You will answer truthfully,' Elise insisted. 'Do you understand me?'

Genevieve's heart began to beat faster, but she nodded.

Elise took her by the hand and led her out of the bedroom and along the landing. Genevieve hastily started to button up her nightdress, but Elise stopped her. 'No,' she whispered, 'leave it like that.'

As they descended the stairs Genevieve didn't notice Elise's self-congratulatory flicker of a smile.

Count de Tranville was fairly drunk. He straightened up at the table as soon as the two lovely girls entered the dining room. Genevieve felt her heart racing. He stared at her blankly, and she was convinced he could see the upper slopes of her breasts through the opening of her nightdress.

Elise took her to within a few feet of him, and he looked at both of them. Elise pulled out a chair for Genevieve - who winced as she carefully placed her sore bottom on it - and then moved round behind him to her place opposite the gingerly sitting girl.

'Um, Genevieve has something to tell you,' she said firmly to her stepfather, without preamble. 'Don't you, Genevieve?'

Genevieve's cheeks turned scarlet. 'I, erm, yes,' she murmured.

'You love me, don't you?' Elise prompted.

'Yes.' Genevieve locked her gaze to her friend, not daring to look at the count's reactions to what was being said. She could feel him staring at her partly naked breasts.

'And there is nothing you'd like better than to share my bed,' Elise continued boldly. 'You would have me do anything to you that I please. Is that not true?'

'Yes.'

'So much so, that even right now you can think of little else but the pleasure I could bring you.'

The count's jaw clenched. He stared at Elise's cool gaze, which was on Genevieve. She was stunning. Her face glowed. Her lips glistened red and looked as soft as rose petals. Her ripe breasts were more appetising than any food.

Elise looked at him and smiled, and then with her eyes returning to Genevieve she began unbuttoning her red dress, and in moments her breasts burst free, voluptuous and irresistible. She held them proudly, her dress slipping down off her shoulders to her elbows. Genevieve's heart pounded and the count gawped like an imbecile.

Elise was naked beneath the dress, her skin glowing healthily. His eyes drank her in, how beautiful she was...

Elise looked at Genevieve. 'Come here,' she beckoned, crooking a finger at her, and the lovely blonde slowly rose from the chair, as though in a trance.

'No,' Elise stopped her, 'don't walk. I want you to crawl to me.'

Genevieve's cheeks burned terribly, both the Count and Elise staring at her. Slowly she dropped to her knees and crawled under the table, and when she emerged on the other side she found herself on her knees between Elise's parted thighs, her curly black pubis glistening invitingly, her elegant fingers toying with her juicy pussy lips.

'Lick me, slave,' she ordered. 'Lick me...'

Her head in a confused spin, Genevieve nodded, glanced over her shoulder at the count, then closed her eyes and moved her face to the succulent, fleshy folds... but before her lips and tongue made contact with their goal the count had risen abruptly from his chair and she was pushed aside.

Like a man possessed he pulled Elise to her feet and spun her round so that her bottom bumped and rested on the edge of the table. Without pausing he pushed open her thighs, and kneeling, began avidly lapping at her pussy as she threw her head back and moaned gutturally, arching her back and thrusting out her breasts.

Genevieve shuffled back, aghast at the debauched scene unravelling before her. The count was like a wild animal, and she could hear the suckling slurps of his lips and tongue amid his avaricious grunts.

Elise's eyes were closed in bliss, and Genevieve rose shakily to her feet. As she did the count spied her from his enviable position between Elise's smooth thighs and grabbed at her, catching the hem of the nightdress as Genevieve jumped back, ripping it a little.

'Come here!' he shouted, his lips glistening wetly as though he'd been gorging on a juicy joint of meat, but Elise cupped his angry face and pulled it to her breasts, where he started lapping and gnawing again. Elise's hands slipped down to his breeches, she unfastened them, and they slipped to his ankles. The count raised his head from her breasts and began kissing her face and throat, his hands clasping her waist.

Genevieve took another hesitant step backwards. The count grabbed Elise and turned her around so that she faced the table, his hands grasping and kneading her buttocks, and then shoved her forward over the table with a heavy thrust that sent bone china plates and silver cutlery scattering, and smashed a crystal wine glass.

Without pausing he clutched her buttocks and thrust his erection into her with one powerful stab of his hips. She stiffened and her mouth opened in a silent scream of mixed joy and shock, the count thrusting so aggressively that Genevieve could hear Elise's middle bumping against the table edge. He grunted and pumped even faster, his face distorted by a fierce snarl of pleasure, beads of sweat trickling from his forehead. Genevieve stepped back further, just as he looked at her.

'Where do you think you're going?' he hissed breathlessly, his jaw tightly clenched. 'I think it's high time you had some of this too, dear girl...'

Genevieve shook her head in denial, unable to speak as she backed further away. Elise cried out, her eyes tightly shut.

De Tranville grasped her wrists, folded them behind her back and held them there, all the time staring into Genevieve's eyes as he fucked his stepdaughter, mocking her... challenging her. She returned his stare for as long as she could, then turned and ran out of the room.

# Chapter Seven

Rodolfo took a clean white shirt from his trunk, flapped it once and spread it over the bed. Claudine and Juliette were getting on his nerves. Increasingly his mind had been turning back to the night he had dinner at Count de Tranville's chateau. He removed the shirt he was wearing ponderously, the image of the young blonde sitting across the dinner table from him on his mind. What a remarkably lovely thing she was.

And yet his lustful eye had flitted from her to the other one, Elise. Perhaps the blonde's shyness made her too much like hard work at a place where he would only spend one night. Time had been short, and the brunette was clearly a safer bet, and as usual his judgement had been proved absolutely correct.

But as he recalled the blonde's eyes, he slowly identified what he could trace there. It was not just girlish innocence, the naïve coyness of a sweet virgin. No, there was something in those eyes that was trying to say something to him, and was at the same time painfully ashamed of what they were trying to say. There was longing; a quietly contained desire that was afraid of itself. Her soul was trying to prise its way out through those sapphire eyes, telling him that she wanted something from him, that she wanted him to take something from her.

Elise, meanwhile, had such a completely different message. Her eyes gazed at him with the knowledge of all the beauty she possessed and an arrogant disregard for whether he appreciated it or not. Her eyes had known pleasures, and rather than be afraid of them, she used them to make herself stronger.

There was a power that radiated from Elise. Her eyes betrayed a soul that was dauntless, obsessed by one thing, whatever it be, and that all other things that stood in the way were like playthings, there for her amusement, pleasure, or curiosity.

She had so coolly sucked his cock that night, so casual, so assured of his readiness, his willingness to participate and enjoy her chosen activity. What if she had not come to his room? Might he have spent more time thinking of the other one? Might he have gone to Genevieve, even just to talk with her, to find out what her eyes tried to hide, what she wanted from him?

He looked back at Claudine and Juliette, a deep frown on his face. He could not wait to return to the Count de Tranville's chateau, he realised. He wanted to see that girl again, to look into the mystery of those eyes that seemed to beg something secret from him, and from him alone...

Rodolfo needed to remain clear in his mind, alert to pursuers. He jumped up beside the coachman and ordered him to ride like the wind to Count de Tranville's chateau.

His eyes glinted brightly in the moonlight and his jaw was so tensely set that the coachman shifted uncomfortably, cursing under his breath each time Rodolfo shouted at him to go faster. With his whip lashing at the four horses they pounded through the dark streets towards the edge of town and the countryside beyond, Rodolfo only too grateful he'd left the burden of the two whores behind when he stealthily rose from their bed and slipped like a phantom from their lodgings. They would only have slowed him down, putting them all at peril, and he was relieved he'd made the right decision.

He regularly turned to peer anxiously over his shoulder into the darkness they left behind, expecting to see a mob giving chase on horseback. He'd heard tell from his sources that the revolutionaries were preparing to pay an imminent visit to Count de Tranville, and he simply had to get there first. No rabble appeared to be in pursuit, but still he bawled at the coachman to make haste, promising to make it worth his while, threatening him if he delayed.

The dangers of the revolution had always been on his mind, but it had never seemed so real or so close as it did now. He was a wanted man. They would try to hunt him down, and if captured they would seek to have him killed without trial or ado.

But how did they know of him? And did they know more? Did they know he was heading to Count de Tranville to escort the count and his two charges out of the country? How could they?

It had to be betrayal. Someone had betrayed him, and perhaps, betrayed them all. But who, and why? They would need to make haste. The longer they stayed the more dangerous it would be for all of them. He stroked the dagger in his inside pocket. It gave him a little comfort to feel the lethal, loyal blade.

He glanced back again, his eyes squinting into the night as he searched the inky-black road and fields behind them. He could have sworn he heard the beat of hooves behind him, but his own coach was moving so fast it was hard to tell. He saw nothing, in any case.

Who had betrayed them? He gazed at the old coachman beside him. Could it have been him? Had he been in town gossiping, talking of his Portuguese master? The old man twitched beneath Rodolfo's scrutiny. He was a wizened but kindly looking soul. Rodolfo shook his head; escape was the only thing to think about now, it was too late and too dangerous to start planning retribution.

It was just after midnight when Rodolfo's coach swung to a halt in front of Count de Tranville's chateau, the horses snorting and sweating heavily, steam rising from their sleekly muscled bodies. He was exhausted too, and like the courageous animals his back was bathed in sweat despite the chill of the night. He patted the coachman's shoulder and sprang down, telling him to be prepared to leave hastily.

With bleary, brooding eyes he thumped impatiently on the front door with his fist, gazing up at the ivy-clad walls of the chateau front. It seemed alluring in its grandeur, but somehow too dark, distant, cold.

There was no response, but Rodolfo thumped noisily again until finally an elderly maid in an old nightgown opened it and smiled at him timidly.

Rodolfo apologised for waking the old lady as he stepped inside and headed straight for the drawing room, where the maid told him she thought her master was, expecting to find the elegant Frenchman and honourable friend of his father enjoying a quiet cigar and a brandy alone, but he was shocked as he knocked and pushed open the door without awaiting a response.

Elise stood there, her arms behind her back. Behind her, draped on a sofa, was Count de Tranville, and their appearance left him curious and speechless.

Elise's lovely face shone brightly, her cheeks glowing, her throat covered in a hot flush. Her sleek black hair hung to her shoulders, slightly dishevelled. She wore the most alluring dress, red silk that clung to her curves, and from the bodice of which her magnificent breasts threatened to spill at any moment. The top two fastenings of the bodice were not fastened, the material straining to contain those luscious breasts, and he got the distinct impression she had hastily slipped the dress on as he stood outside pounding on the front door.

She smiled at him, a replete, mischievous twinkle in her eye. Not sure what to say or do Rodolfo looked to the count, and gawped. Surely it could not be the same man. His white flowing shirt was hanging open, revealing a pale chest. He was shoeless, ruddy of face, and a glassy stupor filled his eyes, like a man who had all his senses so sated that he'd lost his mind.

'Dear Rodolfo, it's been so long since we've had the pleasure,' Elise started coolly. 'You must forgive the appearance of the count and I. We were having a small celebration and were only just getting ready to retire... your visit comes most unexpectedly, Rodolfo. Why, we thought you would not be arriving until tomorrow.'

The young man remained silent for a few moments. How strange a mood the girl seemed to be in. She looked as if she had been caught in a state of intense passion, like one making love, and her tone, why, she sounded more like the man's wife or mistress than his stepdaughter!

'I must beg your forgiveness, too,' he replied slowly, eyeing them both cautiously. 'As you correctly say, I had planned to arrive tomorrow, but somehow it seems the revolutionary committee has caught wind of who I am and I had to escape in haste. Hence, the poverty of my appearance.'

'Rodolfo,' the count mumbled with a slack jaw. 'Is that you?' Through a haze of alcohol the man had only just recognised the new arrival. He made an effort to stand but staggering, thought better of it, and flopped down again. 'Why, this is unexpected,' he groaned. 'Do come and sit down.'

'Sir,' Rodolfo started impatiently, getting more uneasy with every minute that passed, 'there is not much time to lose. I fear that the revolutionaries could be coming here very soon - by as early as tomorrow, perhaps. If we are to leave, we must leave quickly.'

The count gazed vacantly at him without a word or reaction in response to the grave news. He seemed to be in a trance, as if not hearing what had just been said, let alone grasping the enormity of it. Rodolfo frowned in frustration.

'My stepfather is exhausted,' Elise said. 'He's also a little the worse for drink at the moment.'

Rodolfo gazed at her, stunned by the apparent lack of concern either showed for the graveness of their situation.

'Why, you also look exhausted,' she went on in a cool, hushed tone.

Rodolfo needed to rouse the count, but the man was clearly in no state for action.

'I believe it might be best if you get some rest,' Elise suggested, ignoring his agitation. 'We can assess our predicament in the morning, when we are all feeling refreshed and able to make pertinent decisions. And my stepfather has made some changes to his plans of which he will need to inform you. But it must wait until tomorrow, when we are all rested and ready.'

Rodolfo nodded; perhaps she was right. They had a little time, he assessed, and with the count in such a state, and with his own exhaustion making him edgy and perhaps clouding his judgment it was probably better to take the opportunity to snatch a few hours' rest. Hopefully the count would have sobered up by dawn and they could start out then. He smiled politely to Elise and agreed with her, accepting her offer of a bed for the night.

'Come,' she beckoned, leading him by the hand, 'let me show you to your room. I will come back and help my stepfather up to his bedchamber once you are settled.'

He followed the enticing beauty up the stairs and along the dimly lit landing, taking a moment to forget their troubles and instead enjoying the view of her temptingly swaying bottom within the red silk dress. He suddenly thought of Genevieve. Where was she? Asleep in her bed, no doubt. They stopped at a closed door.

'Your room,' Elise purred, her tone dripping with sultry suggestion. 'It's the same one you slept in the last time you stayed here... do you remember that...?'

He smiled. 'Of course, how could I ever forget it?'

Elise pursed her rouged lips and gazed fleetingly down at his groin, the tip of her tongue appearing for a moment, then back up into his dark eyes. Then she smiled and bid him goodnight, taking him aback somewhat, leaving him wishing he'd pulled her into the bedroom with him as he watched her drift elegantly back towards the stairs.

Exhausted, Rodolfo did not bother to undress. Instead he threw himself heavily across the bed and closed his tired eyes, exulting in the feel of his tensed and knotted muscles at last finding a little time to relax. Soon he drifted off to sleep...

He awoke shortly after. There were noises outside his room. He lay with his eyes open for a while, breathing silently - listening intently.

There were whispered female voices, fading in the direction of the stairs. He rose slowly, not wanting to make any noise that might give away his state of wakefulness. Carefully he moved like a shadow to the door, pulled it ajar, and listened again.

The whispers were heading down the stairs, so he opened the door and slipped out, heading after them.

The hall below was in darkness, just a narrow beam of light from the slightly ajar door of the drawing room piercing the gloom. The voices became louder as he crept down, and were now joined by the deeper tones of the count. He stepped to the door, put a hand flat against it, and peered into the room.

Count de Tranville looked more aware of his surroundings now, and was seated with a little more decorum than before, although the wine was clearly still flowing freely, the red contents of a crystal glass slopping precariously in one hand as he belched and gazed loosely at Elise and another girl, both standing quietly before him, their backs to the door from where Rodolfo lurked in shadow. The count chuckled drunkenly, lewdly.

Elise still wore the red dress that made her so enticing to the eye, and the other girl wore nothing more than a simple white nightdress, her golden hair caressing her shoulders... but what really caught Rodolfo's eye was the curtain cord that bound her wrists behind her back, her dainty hands resting together on the upper slopes of her pert bottom!

It was dear Genevieve, he realised.

The count's head wobbled a little as he slurped more wine, his lips struggling to find the rim of the glass, his tongue protruding and helping them locate it but not before some spilled onto his shirtfront.

'What sport have we now, Elise?' he asked, slurring slightly, his eyes struggling to stay fully open, one more than the other. With his free hand he lewdly rubbed the evident lump in his lap.

Elise smiled. 'Well,' she started, 'you now know fully what Genevieve's tastes are. As your dutiful stepdaughter I've done my best to show you that she feels nothing for men, to save you from making a fool of yourself by persisting with this foolish idea of proposing marriage to her.'

The count sighed and nodded, taking another slurp of wine at the same time and spilling more or the red liquid down his front as a consequence. 'Bring her here,' he ordered, and even from where he stood unseen, Rodolfo noted the glint of triumph in Elise's eyes as she took the poor girl's arm and led her close to the sitting count.

'Get over my knee,' the inebriated count demanded, and despite struggling slightly with her hands tied, Genevieve succumbed to the dominating influence of Elise and lowered herself over his thighs, balancing uncomfortably, just her toes in contact with the carpet.

'I will now punish you for your unnatural desires,' announced the drunken hypocrite, looking down at the pretty bottom over his lap, savouring her gentle weight moving imperceptibly on the straining lump in his breeches.

Elise slipped onto the sofa beside him. 'Go ahead, sir,' she urged. 'I've brought her here for you, for the very purpose of trying to beat some of your honourable principals and authority into her wayward soul.'

She slipped a hand between the shapely hip of the prone girl and his belly, locating his hidden erection and rubbing it encouragingly. He stared deep into her eyes, his lips hanging slack and making him look like an imbecile as he took two attempts to place his wine glass on the occasional table beside him.

Without taking her eyes from his, Elise fumbled open his breeches and pulled out his cock, throbbing in her cool fist. 'Beat her,' she whispered.

He looked down at the girl's bottom before him and kneaded it roughly. Then, raising his palm, he swiftly brought it down on the hidden cheeks.

Genevieve squealed and her feet kicked, making the count smile and look at Elise, who was smiling back at him. She moved her lips closer to his, her hand still massaging his cock. 'Again,' she whispered.

De Tranville repeated the blow, this time with greater intensity. Genevieve winced and kicked again.

'She likes it,' Elise whispered to him, goading him to greater efforts, grasping his cock more firmly. 'Do it again.'

De Tranville let his palm slam down again, and as it struck Elise jerked his cock more firmly, leaving him on the very verge of an ejaculation.

'That's it,' Elise murmured. 'Again... again...'

De Tranville allowed his head to reel back, a look of deep satisfaction gripping his face as his stepdaughter masturbated him and the gorgeous blonde girl squirmed on his lap. He panted, ready to explode at any moment.

'Do you see what fun we could have together?' Elise whispered in his ear, and he let his hand rest on Genevieve's delightful bottom, enjoying the feel of her flesh beneath the cotton nightdress as he mauled her.

'If you'd only agree to marry Madame Coubette,' Elise continued in his ear. 'Every day would be like this. You could still have her, and me, and Genevieve. We would not have to run away.'

De Tranville flexed his shoulders and brought his palm down again on Genevieve's bottom. She winced, her hip bumping softly against Elise's fist and his standing erection.

'You might be right,' he grunted, clenching his jaw and trying to prolong his pleasure.

Rodolfo had seen and heard enough. He hadn't put his life at risk to save the count and his family from the revolution, only to have depravity and debauchery put him at even further risk.

With his eyes on the count and Elise he stepped out from behind the cover of the door and placed himself directly in front of them.

'Rodolfo,' Elise started angrily. 'I thought you were sleeping.'

'I was... I woke up,' he said abruptly. He looked at Genevieve, and then his hand moved to the back of his waistband and a small dagger emerged. He reached towards Genevieve's bound wrists and sliced through the cords, then taking her by the arm, he helped her to her feet.

Silence filled the room, and the count looked at the younger man with dazed irritation. His cock was still standing tall from his opened breeches, but its keenness had waned. He seemed to be awaiting some sort of explanation as to why his fun had been interrupted.

Rodolfo's eyes were fixed firmly on Genevieve, and she stood wide-eyed, gawping at him in confusion. She felt a dark heat throbbing in her pussy. It was him!

A sob broke from her throat. She burst into tears, wrapped her arms round his neck for a fleeting second, then turned and fled upstairs. Rodolfo watched her go.

Elise frowned at him coldly. 'How dare you brandish that thing in here!' she snapped, indicating the knife. 'You're nothing but a foreign rogue!'

Rodolfo put the dagger back in his waistband. 'I apologise,' he said politely, despite beginning to lower his opinion of the two sitting before him, 'but these are dangerous times.'

Elise continued to glare at him.

'My father has offered you his hospitality and security, given the dangers that are surrounding you here in France,' Rodolfo went on. 'I will be leaving at first light. If you still choose to avail of my father's offer, please be ready to depart with me. If you are not ready, I shall return to Portugal alone.'

He looked at the count. 'I can only hope that you are sober and in command of yourself by then, sir,' he added curtly.

'Why, you cheeky young bastard!' de Tranville roared indignantly, trying to rise from the sofa, but Elise held his arm and stopped him. Rodolfo gazed at her for a moment, then turned and headed upstairs.

There was a tap at the door. Genevieve had buried her face in the pillows, her buttocks still burning from the count's spanking. She had kicked aside the bedding, trying to cool the scorched globes.

'Leave me alone,' she sulked, but the door edged open anyway and a man entered. It was Rodolfo. She gasped, turned and pulled the sheet over herself as he moved closer and sat on the edge of the bed.

'Are you all right?' he asked compassionately, and she nodded. 'What was that all about?'

Genevieve looked deeply into his shadowed eyes, and shrugged.

'You're tired?' he asked further. 'I'm sorry, I just needed to see you, to make sure you're all right.'

'Where did you go?' she muttered sadly. 'I've thought about you a lot since we first met.'

'And I've thought about you, too,' Rodolfo confessed truthfully.

'Elise told me about you, and your philandering. She told me what happened between the two of you the last time you stayed here. She told me I wasn't the type of girl for you.'

'I've learned that Elise is a conniving bitch,' Rodolfo whispered, and then placed his hands on her shoulders, pulled her to him and kissed her. She closed her eyes and melted into the sensual embrace.

'So much has happened to me since that night,' Genevieve told him. 'I've been so confused. Count de Tranville wants to marry me, but Elise has been trying to make him change his mind.'

'Do you want to marry him?'

Genevieve shook her head, resting her cheek into his cupped palm. 'I'm not a child, you know,' she whispered, looking up at him. 'I'm a woman, and I know how to please a man.'

'What are you saying?'

'I haven't ever been with a man, but I...'

'You don't even know me,' he said, anticipating her meaning.

'When I first saw you I felt I had needed you all my life. As if you were what my life was waiting for.'

Rodolfo smiled and kissed her again...

Suddenly there was a loud crash and a thud and the door burst open. Something whistled viciously through the air, and as Rodolfo looked round in surprise the leather riding-crop slashed across his face. He yelled and clasped his cheek, but the leather whistled again and bit cruelly into his other cheek.

'Brazen whore!' a voice bawled. 'Duplicitous little slattern!'

Count de Tranville stood by the bed, his shirt hanging open, his face red and his chest heaving as he loomed aggressively over both of them, clutching the whip in his fist. His bloodshot eyes bulged and spittle dribbled from one corner of his slack lips, giving him the look of an insane man. He raised the crop again, this time to strike Genevieve. 'So you don't like men, eh?' he snarled. 'Or is it just *me* your whorish pussy objects to? After everything I've done for you, you ungrateful little?!'

Rodolfo's dagger flashed upward from behind his back and with a deceptively innocuous thud embedded itself deep in the drunken assailant's chest. He gawped, the tirade of abuse dying in his throat, his expression one of surprise rather than pain. Rodolfo pulled the dagger back out and a dark red stain, almost black in the half-light, started spreading on the count's white shirt. He gazed at Genevieve, his eyes unblinking but now filled with disbelief, his features frozen as though sculpted from stone.

An aching pounding erupted in Genevieve's head, a rhythmic beating as if fists were smashing against wood, resonating dully inside her skull.

The wounded man fell clumsily on top of them, but Rodolfo struggled with his bulk and eased him to the floor beside the bed.

The thumping continued, and then it seemed like something was splintering and crashing. Genevieve could hear Elise running along the landing, calling down to the elderly staff who could now be heard scurrying around in the hall, frantically running from room to room and calling for their master, the count.

'He left me no choice,' Rodolfo said to Genevieve. 'You saw that, didn't you? The drunken fool left me no choice.'

Genevieve nodded, barely able to grasp what was happening. All hell had broken loose in the chateau around them.

Rodolfo leapt to his feet. 'They're breaking down the front door,' he said urgently, and then ran out to the landing, leaning on the balustrade to scan the scene below. 'I knew it,' he scowled, his jaw clenched. 'They're here.'

Without wasting a second he dashed back into the bedroom, shut the door and wedged a chair beneath the handle. 'They're here,' he repeated earnestly to Genevieve. 'We've got to get away. The revolutionaries are here!'

Genevieve was reaching out tentatively and touching the count's arm, trying to offer some help or comfort but uncertain of what she was doing or what on earth was happening. The count was muttering unintelligibly, his voice no more than a wheezing rasp in his throat, blood coating his teeth.

'Come on,' Rodolfo snapped, pulling the kneeling girl to her feet. 'We've got to leave the damned obstinate fool.'

'But,' Genevieve protested, 'he's been good to me. We can't just leave him here like this, to die.'

'He's brought it upon himself.' Rodolfo moved to the window like a fleeting shadow in the half-light, unlatched it and stared down.

Heavy footsteps were charging up the stairs outside the bedroom, and then the door began crashing beneath the onslaught of clubs and fists, gruff male voices shouting and barking orders to others as the chair wedged beneath the door handle threatened to shatter and break before the desperate couple had a chance to escape.

'Quick, do as I say!' Rodolfo yelled at Genevieve, trying to snap her out of her torpor. 'Do you trust me?'

'Yes,' she murmured, as though in a dream, so he swung her round, dragged the heavy mattress off the bed and managed to shove it out of the window. 'Good, then let's go!'

With a lunge he raised her in his arms and swung her so that she clung around his shoulders. He then clambered through the window and clasping vines of ivy began struggling down, but it was slow going and he could hear the bedroom door was on the point of yielding to the battering, so he had no choice but to close his eyes and let go...

'Damnation!' he groaned venomously, lying on his back on the strategically dropped mattress, Genevieve sprawled across his chest. 'I think I've broken every bone in my entire body.'

She clutched him, her eyes wide and brimming with tears and terror. The thudding sound continued, but it was her heart this time. It was racing so fast she was sure it was ready to burst.

'Their wagons must be at the front,' he whispered as they rose stiffly and quickly checked for any damaged limbs. 'You stay here,' he ordered, 'I'll be straight back,' and before Genevieve could beg him to stay with her he disappeared silently into the darkness.

Genevieve hid down in the flowerbed that hid her, but the sound of the bedroom door above giving way, and her concerns for the welfare of Rodolfo, made her dash after him.

Around the corner of the chateau she spied two armed men beside a convoy of three wagons. Sitting on one of the vehicles was a driver, and the three of them were looking towards the shattered front door. Already Rodolfo was stealthily stalking them, approaching from behind and slightly to the side, his dagger glinting menacingly in the moonlight.

He was close when one of the men turned and cried, the blade flashed and the man clutched his throat, slumping to his knees. The second man tried to raise his musket as the driver shouted and jumped to the ground. The dagger slashed again and sank into the second man's chest and he slumped too, his hands clamped over the wound. But the numbers proved too much and the driver jumped onto Rodolfo's back before he could strike a third time.

Genevieve felt as though her heart was exploding. Nothing seemed real. She ran to help, terrified of the man on top of Rodolfo and what he might do. They were wrestling. The driver was overweight but he was hurting her man, pounding him with punches to the back of his head. She screamed.

'Be quiet!' Rodolfo gasped from under the man. 'Hit him with something!' Panicking, Genevieve tried to grab the man by the shoulders and wrestle him off Rodolfo. The wounded revolutionary, lying nearby clutching his chest, stared at her in disbelief.

'Fuck...' he muttered, distracting Rodolfo's assailant, and in that instant the dagger struck again. The assailant cursed and rolled to the side, and Rodolfo struggled up and kicked the man in the stomach, making him groan again and curl up defensively.

Rodolfo stared at the man on his back, his face contorted in agony as he held his wounded chest. 'Don't hurt me please, sir,' he begged, a terrified smile making him grimace.

Rodolfo bent over the body of the dead one and hurriedly hauled off his boots, breeches, shirt, topcoat and hat, and threw them into the nearest wagon.

'Get up!' he ordered Genevieve, pushing her into the back and throwing the clothes at her. 'Put these on,' he told her.

The overweight driver rolled onto his side, clutching his wounded shoulder, and watched Rodolfo as he clambered onto the wagon and lashed at the horses. 'Stop them!' he yelled. 'Someone, they're getting away!'

The horses broke into an immediate gallop and the wagon lurched away down the drive.

'D-did you see her?' the man with the chest wound groaned to his overweight associate.

'I did,' the driver muttered, checking the damage to his shoulder and realising it was not much more than a bad cut. 'Aye, I did, and I'll fuck the slut harder than she's ever been fucked when we catch them... the bastards.'

'I - I don't think I'll have the chance to,' the man with the chest wound gasped, and then coughed. 'I'm not going to make it. Just be sure to fuck that cute little arse of hers for me, if...'

# Chapter Eight

Elise awoke to an unpleasantly acrid smell and numbness in her left cheek. She blinked a few times and yawned, wincing as she felt a sudden pain in her jaw. She touched it tentatively, making her wince again.

Curiously she was draped in a thick woollen cloak. It felt itchy and she scratched her arms a few times. She tried to sit up but gasped in surprise, for she was lying on stone slabs, cold and abrasive. Her fingers grasped rough straw, and her left buttock and thigh were as numb as her cheek.

Beneath the cloak she was almost naked, only covered by one of her white shifts, which was now grimy and stained.

'Get her up!' a gruff voice ordered.

Straw clung to her black hair, which hung loosely around her shoulders. She brushed at it, about to turn over, but there were footsteps coming towards her. Two stocky men approached and lifted her onto her unsteady feet.

'Gently!' the voice commanded, and she shook them off determinedly. 'Leave her!' The voice added.

Elise looked around. She was in a dingy, damp cell, and it was cold. Beneath a small barred window, from which dull grey daylight seeped, there was a chair and a desk, behind which hulked a man, another beside him with his back against the wall.

'Come here,' the man behind the desk beckoned. They were both sullen, a fresh-looking scar marking the cheek of one who spoke to her. She moved to the desk, feeling chilly, her thighs and shoulders aching. 'Take a seat,' he ordered. 'I've been waiting for you to wake up, Elise de Tranville. You've had a long sleep. Have a drink.'

There was a bowl of water on the desk in front of her, so she sat on the vacant chair and drank thirstily.

'I have some bad news for you, and some good news,' the man behind the desk went on. He held a riding-crop and swished it casually through the air. 'Which would you prefer first?'

Elise stared at him. He was a tall man with grey hair. He had sharp features and a long nose, his complexion slightly pockmarked. His eyes were dull, lifeless. She glanced at the crop. It was Count de Tranville's.

'Well, the bad news first, I suppose,' he answered for her, smiling, his teeth looking sharp, like those of a rat. 'Bad news for you, at least, but not for the revolution.'

'What is it?' Elise snapped impatiently. Her head hurt.

'Your stepfather is dead.'

She stared at him coldly. He rubbed his nose with a bony finger and gazed at her coolly.

'He died of the wound inflicted by Rodolfo de Agora before our surgeons could do anything to help him.' The man smiled and looked down. 'And before he could be tried for his treachery.'

Elise's eyes watered slightly; she did not want to cry in front of this loathsome creature.

'That was a nasty knock you received,' the man went on, watching her closely. 'You've been unconscious for over a day. I'm sorry my men were a little boisterous, but they couldn't afford to put themselves at risk. You understand, I'm sure.'

'Where are they?' Elise asked, feeling sick at the realisation that her stepfather was dead. 'Where are Rodolfo and Genevieve?'

'Ah,' the man sighed. 'Now, that is a very good question. One that I was hoping you could help me with.'

Elise stared at him blankly. What was he planning to do to her?

'But first that piece of good news I promised you.' He smiled in a way that disconcerted Elise. 'It seems you have a friend in a high place who thinks very highly of you. A certain Madame Coubette. According to her, you are an ardent supporter of the revolution and you are willing to assist us in any way you can.'

He looked at Elise quizzically, and she felt compelled to lower her eyes.

'She has requested that no harm come to you,' he continued. 'She wants to take you home to help you recover, but I need to keep you here for questioning,' he smiled in a way that made her shudder, 'for a while, at least.'

Elise remained silent.

'You're very lucky, you know,' he went on. 'If it wasn't for her insistence on your revolutionary ideals, you would not only be sharing the same fate as all other aristocrats, but I would make your punishment a matter of personal pleasure.' He slammed the crop down on the table with a loud snap, making Elise flinch where she sat. He chuckled, bending the crop in his hands, smirking through his sharp teeth. 'What a strange bunch you aristocrats are,' he sniggered, staring at her coldly.

Elise noted tightness setting into his jaw. She felt warmth filling her cheeks, a tingling in her nipples, but she stoically fixed her eyes on his. 'If Madame Coubette, your high-placed friend, has expressed a wish for me not to be harmed,' she said, as calmly as she could manage, 'I would suggest you do as she says.'

The man remained silent, but still the inquisitor's glaring eyes did not flicker from her face, and she couldn't help but notice the intensity with which his fingers gripped the crop, the implement forming a slim leather arc between his two fists, and she wondered at the wisdom of goading him. He was clearly very volatile and very dangerous.

'Monsieur Coubette and his wife have been very generous and very useful to me,' he said, so quietly Elise could barely hear him. But there was menace in his cold tone. 'He has donated considerable funds to our cause, and she has extended numerous services of all kinds. However, I am the head of Rency's revolutionary committee, and let me warn you that if you provoke me I shall whip you like a cur, regardless of what our bourgeois friends request.'

The man was in control again. Elise's cloak had slipped open slightly, and he casually glanced down a little, blatantly admiring the upper slopes of her creamy breasts and the beckoning shadows of her deep cleavage. He drew his tongue pensively over his upper lip and looked back up into her eyes. He was mocking her again.

'While you have been sleeping,' he went on, 'Madame Coubette and I have been discussing you at length. You, and your future.' Elise thought it wise to remain silent. Perhaps she shouldn't push him too much too soon.

'What do you know about this man Rodolfo?' he asked sharply.

'He is Portuguese,' Elise told him without compunction; she felt nothing but loathing towards the man who had murdered her stepfather, and would rejoice on the imminent day when the guillotine took his head. 'He is a man of leisure, an aristocrat. He was planning to take my stepfather and me to Portugal. I didn't want to go, of course.'

'Where is he now?'

'I expect he's making his way out of the country, as planned.' Elise shrugged. 'He may have already parted with Genevieve, to save his own worthless skin.'

'Genevieve de Montvert?' the man probed curiously, and then smiled. It was an icy smile, a smile that made even Elise shudder. 'It is strange,' he went on, as though thinking aloud, 'but it is clear that Madame Coubette harbours a hatred for this Genevieve de Montvert.'

'I know exactly how she feels,' Elise muttered, and the man observed her silently, his dead eyes once more flitting down to her smooth slopes of bared flesh.

'Personal feelings aren't my business,' he said firmly. 'But spies are.'

Elise frowned with puzzlement.

'I believe this Rodolfo is in touch with other aristocrats in France, as well as their sympathisers. I believe he passes funds to those with cause to interfere with the revolution. I also believe he intends to continue with his activities, despite his near capture.'

As he spoke Elise followed the movement of the man's eyes, crawling over those areas of her flesh that were naked to him. She felt her lascivious ripples stiffen and pulled the cloak tighter so that their outline could be seen through the rough fabric, deciding it would be much wiser to have the man as an ally rather than an enemy.

The sight of her sultry beauty was clearly distracting him, so she smiled invitingly and crossed her legs, allowing the cloak to slip apart, baring her slender thighs. He stared down for a moment, and then lifted his eyes back to hers.

'It is for these reasons that I want Rodolfo de Agora to be located and captured,' he continued, as though unmoved by her beauty. 'Captured or killed, either will suffice.'

Elise smiled alluringly. 'It is a commendable ambition, sir,' she purred in hushed tones. 'And one that would make me very happy, too. I would have nothing but the highest regard for the man responsible for instigating the operation. He would have my undying gratitude and admiration. He would be a man worthy of my most sincere affections...'

'Madame Coubette believes that you might be able and willing to help me with this objective,' he went on, his penis hardening under the desk as he interpreted her innuendos correctly.

Elise remained silent, but absently smoothed a hand over her thighs.

'According to her you are able to facilitate his capture, and as a bonus, the capture of Genevieve de Montvert, either in France or wherever they hide like the vermin they are.' He watched her hand gliding over her thighs. 'In exchange for your assistance you will be freed. You will also be entitled to keep a proportion of your property.'

Elise frowned. 'What do you mean?' she asked.

'Your stepfather's chateau and goods have been confiscated by the revolution,' he answered blankly. 'However, there are certain debts that we have owing to Monsieur Coubette. In part exchange for the write-off of these debts we are handing over fifty percent of the estate to his wife. The other fifty percent will be given to you in exchange for your services; this one I have just mentioned, and those that either myself, others in the committee or Monsieur and Madame Coubette may from time to time call on you to perform.'

Elise grimaced, her eyes staring at him coldly.

'But relax,' he said slowly. 'As far as I am concerned, the capture of Rodolfo is the only real service I want from you. And if it happens that in some way you can help with the capture of other traitors, then I may call on you further.'

Her lips were still tightly clenched.

'As far as Madame Coubette is concerned,' he continued. 'Well, she is well known for her fiery temper, a temper so strong that it often clouds her wisdom. As we spoke she swore that if you could offer her Genevieve de Montvert as a prize, she would well consider returning her half of the estate to you. It is something I'm sure you two can discuss together. I believe she is coming this afternoon to invite you to enjoy her hospitality at her home. Her hospitality is splendid, I can assure you.'

The man stood up to leave, and Elise stood up too.

'I hope we understand each other, Elise de Tranville,' he said, and then without warning his eyes narrowed and with the speed of a snake he snatched her wrist and spun her round. Elise could only offer a staccato shriek under the speed and surprise of the attack, unable to offer any resistance as he twisted and pinned her arm excruciatingly up behind her back. The desk bumped against her thighs as he breathed down her neck and leant his weight against her, pushing her down flat over the rough wood and ripping off the cloak, which he dropped to the grimy floor. Her cotton shift rucked up, leaving her bottom bared, and she grimaced as her breasts squashed painfully against the wooden surface, his weight pressing her down.

Then with a sudden crack she felt a scorching strip bite across her exposed buttocks. She wanted to yell her outrage, but held it in as terror blended with a treacherous heat simmering between her legs, warming her insides, making her heart pound and her breath catch in her lungs.

With one hand still twisting her arm the man slashed the crop down onto her bottom again. She bit her lip against the pain, her sex rubbing against the edge of the desk. She whimpered lamely. He struck again, turning the stripes of scorching heat into a generalised spread of warmth all over her rounded bottom cheeks. Her pussy pulsed heatedly, growing increasingly wet. Her mind spun, and she saw herself back on the dinning table, her buttocks proffered to her stepfather, and she wanted it again. She wanted something to fill her now, to throb deep inside her and make her rock back and forth as her pleasure rose to new heights. And she wanted Genevieve there to witness her ecstasy. She wanted to live that ecstatic night again.

'Fuck me...' she urged hoarsely. 'Please, fuck me as hard as you can...'

But the man needed no invitation. His erection was already in his hand. It thrust into her, filling her with one long penetration and drilling deep into her molten centre. She moaned, mumbling deliriously to herself, her eyes tightly closed as she absorbed the joy of being roughly fucked by the loathsome brute.

He pumped angrily, watching the girl's perfect fleshy spheres quiver and listening to the slap of his hairy groin against them as he inexorably quickened his rhythm. She fucked like a whore, he mused, rutting even more aggressively against her.

Elise felt her nipples harden and rub painfully through her shift against the desk. Her legs were shaking, leaving her barely able to hold herself up, especially when he let go of her wrist and clasped her buttocks with both hands, kneading them like dough. He grunted like a wild boar, still rutting furiously, his rod ploughing deep inside her.

And then he pressed deeper than ever and slumped, exhausted, onto her back, his cock pulsing rhythmically as it discharged his load, some seeping back and trickling down the insides of her thighs. She lay beneath his weight, panting, savouring her own diminishing waves of pleasure, her mind still reliving the recent night when her stepfather had fucked her in similar fashion, right in front of Genevieve.

The man refastened his breeches. The riding-crop was on the floor, so he stooped and picked it up, glancing at Elise the whole time. Then he opened the heavy wooden door and left her alone in the silence and gloom, tears suddenly blurring her vision and meandering down her cheeks.

# Chapter Nine

There was too much confusion going on in Genevieve's mind. She had wanted Rodolfo from the first moment she ever set eyes on him, and she still did, didn't she?

She knew there was no one else like him. But during the period they had spent together he seemed removed from the man she imagined him to be. She was surprised and uncertain of his ruthlessness.

So much had happened to her in so short a time. Things of all kinds flashed through her mind all through the day, and more so while she slept in her bedchamber in the craggy, hillside home of the Conde de Agora, near the ancient town of Sintra, some twenty miles from Lisbon.

Their flight from France had exhausted every nerve in her body. After fleeing from de Tranville's chateau she found herself crying uncontrollably as she struggled into the dead man's clothes and as Rodolfo shouted and lashed furiously at the horses.

Through the night they bumped along a deeply rutted forest path, and once clear of it he took them across fields and manoeuvred from one track to the next for the whole of the following day. He seemed to want to stop only briefly, and only then for the sake of the horses.

Somehow she managed to sleep intermittently on the wagon floor, although each time they stopped she felt every inch of her body aching.

At times he was taciturn. He said they would need to stay away from towns, so hungry and dirty they would sit by a wood fire at night, and she would nestle into his brawny arms for warmth and fear of the dark and the outdoors. But, as close as she was to him, she would stay awake wondering what would happen to her if he slept too deeply to hear the night's dangers. It seemed as if she had never slept at all.

There were times when he would simply ignore her and wander off with the musket he had quickly snatched after the fight, leaving her alone and terrified, returning hours later with a string of dead birds. He would pluck and roast them and avidly they would feed their aching stomachs like savages. He would smile as they chewed on the rough birds together, almost as if he were enjoying himself.

Guessing routes, they arrived at the port of La Rochelle in what must have been about three or four days, but the time seemed to have merged into one long painful blur to Genevieve.

In his way he had been considerate and oversaw her survival in the wild, but there were times when she thought surrender would be preferable to the painfully buffeting ride, the vigils for pursuers, the sleepless nights, the diet of little more than roast wildfowl, berries and water, and then the voyage to come.

They were filthy as he pulled her along the harbour jetty, chatting, bartering with or simply talking down to scruffy captains as if he still were the fine gentleman and dandy and not a desperate man on the run.

He would switch from one language or dialect to another, at times remonstrating with his arms and shouting like a street vendor, at times making her wince with the crudeness of his colloquy and vulgarity. The mariners seemed to come from all over the place - Frenchmen, Spaniards, Italians and Greeks. He treated them all with the same mix of bluster and camaraderie.

Rodolfo's jaw was covered in dark stubble, and sweat and soil clung to his clothes and forehead. He had almost no money in his purse, and after watching him spend nearly all of it on food and wine for them both in a seedy, whore-filled inn, she watched him sell the horses and wagon for a fraction of their value to a total stranger there.

As the man trundled off, singing happily, her heart sank to new depths and tears filled her eyes. The sight of their departing transport reminded her that there was no return for her to the place she had called home. Where would she end up now?

With the money from the sale he negotiated a pricey passage to Portugal from a small, highly dangerous looking man who would not take his eyes from her as they bartered over the fare. Finally, rubbing his chin and winking from her to one of his bearded and toothless crewmen, he agreed.

She remained silent throughout, close behind the dishevelled man who had once been the one of her dreams, terrified of the dangerous faces that seemed to bode her nothing but ill will.

The grubby man was a Portuguese sea captain, and almost as soon as they had set sail a heated argument erupted between him and Rodolfo outside their shoddy cabin, all over something she did not understand.

They harangued each other in Portuguese for a lengthy period, and towards the end the voices of three of the ship's equally menacing crew joined in, and she could perceive that threats and curses were being exchanged. At one point there was a thumping and stumbling sound, followed by curses and shouts.

But amazingly it seemed to all end with laugher, and the voices of Rodolfo, the captain and the crewmen faded up onto deck. Rodolfo returned some hours later, fairly drunk and with a purplish bruise around one slightly swollen eye.

He only explained it to her afterwards, though, casually and with a burst of laughter, once they had arrived in safety and spent a few days resting at his father's hillside home.

The captain and crew had taken Genevieve, with her clear eyes and slender shape, her grubbiness, her long hair hidden up under a hat and man's clothes, to be a harbour rent boy. The captain's own cherished cabin boy, a former rent boy from Marseilles, had run away while the ship was in port and the captain wanted Genevieve to take his place. He insisted that he had given them such a low passage fare on the assumption of Rodolfo's consent to this arrangement.

The argument only ended when Rodolfo finally explained that Genevieve was, in fact, a young Frenchwoman and his bride to be. Into the bargain, he told the man that they were desperate lovers and were eloping, so to escape her overbearing parents she had needed the disguise.

But, with the revelation that Rodolfo's companion was a girl and not a boy, the captain had immediately lost interest in the reasons for why they appeared as they did, the argument ended immediately and after much backslapping he and the mariners became drinking comrades.

Apparently, Rodolfo told Genevieve, the captain had once been unhappily married to an unfaithful slut who filled her bed each night with a different man while he was at sea, and he had been at sea for so many years and known some many wicked trollops in so many ports, that he had long lost interest in women altogether. So, over many bottles of wine he had sorely bemoaned the loss of his cabin boy - who was occasionally shared with his equally lonely crew.

Getting regularly drunk on wine, the seafaring fellow amazed Rodolfo by somehow managing to get them safely to Lisbon, although that may have been more a matter of luck than good seamanship, Rodolfo admitted to Genevieve, for once already at sea he'd noticed a deep crack ran all the way up the main mast that could have caused it to snap clean away at any point during the rough voyage. And rats had left most of the ship's ropes and sails threadbare, but despite all this he and the captain got along well together.

The captain tried to make Rodolfo promise that if he were ever returning to France, he would sail with him. Rodolfo agreed, and he, for his part, promised that if he ever happened to cross paths with any handsome rent boys on the Lisbon streets that longed to go to sea, he would make sure they got in touch with the good captain.

The captain took his offer seriously and kissed him on both cheeks and clasped his hands. He told Rodolfo that he would be staying in port for several weeks. He intended to get his ship repaired, to chase up money owed to him for old deliveries and to find love and companionship for his lonely seafaring days.

They bade farewell to each other, and the captain showed a sudden politeness to Genevieve. With her hat removed and the soil and sweat wiped from her face, he could now see what an extremely fine and unmistakeably female girl she was. In a strange dialect of French, he apologised profusely for his misunderstanding and kissed her hands.

It was on the boat that Rodolfo had declared his intentions to marry her. He had watched over her as she slept, pitying her dire state and complete exhaustion. He had let her take the bunk all the time, and dabbed her hot face with a damp cloth. And each time she looked at him and his bright eyes shining from his dirty face, she felt more and more love for him despite her uncertainties. But so much had happened in so short a period that she needed time. She could not marry him until all her thoughts and emotions had somehow found rest, and it was because of all these distractions that the wonderful view from her window at Conde de Agora's home made little impression on her. The fresh air and the sight of lush forested valleys and hills beneath blue skies only seemed to increase her melancholy.

Recurrently she would wake up panting and sweating. In her dreams she would keep seeing Count de Tranville towering above her, blood spreading from his chest, his bulging eyes fixed on hers in a mixture of disbelief, horror, accusing, and awareness of his own end.

She had grown to dislike him and his insistence on marrying her, despite her objections. She had grown to be afraid of him and his intentions. But how much were Madame Coubette and Elise responsible for the man's state of mind and behaviour?

Did Rodolfo really have to kill him? What sort of a man could take another's life without hesitating? And then only minutes later he had killed another man and possibly two more in cold blood.

In the darkness of sleepless nights she would see Rodolfo squatting at a fire as he had during their flight, brooding in the dark woods, a dead bird's blood staining his killer hands, his fingers plucking the feathers without him even having to look down.

He had lied, too, or as good as lied, to his own father. Having reached the safety of their destination she washed and then slept for almost a night and a day. Then over dinner she met the Conde de Agora, an imposing man, as tall and dark as his son, but with a stately belly and a sincere, wrinkled face. He had looked at them both with great fondness and, with concern, immediately asked after the welfare of his friend, Count de Tranville, and his daughter Elise.

Without hesitation or compulsion Rodolfo informed him that the count had been killed while bravely trying to escape capture, a victim of France's terrible revolution, and that Elise was captured before he could do anything to help and was probably in prison. And then he changed the subject.

It was as if what he had done simply no longer mattered. As though he had dismissed it from his mind. His attention turned instead to the welfare of his three brothers, all serving as officers in the army.

He was the youngest of the four, and humorously remarked that it was as well that they were away from home, for in all likelihood they would otherwise start bullying him as usual, and probably end up proposing and then duelling for the hand of fair

Genevieve.

His father looked sternly on him and asked if he had not been reading his letters. Rodolfo had not received any for seven or eight months, he explained, so his father nodded and related the events that Rodolfo had clearly missed.

The French Revolution had sent shivers down the spines of all the Portuguese monarchy, as it had done to all the monarchs of Europe. Queen Maria I was said to have had constant nightmares and lost her sanity in the wake of the death of the French king, Louis XVI.

The previous year, the year of 1793, Portugal had signed a treaty of mutual assistance with Britain and Spain, and with it had sent six thousand troops to join the Spanish army in an attack on Southern France. All three of his brothers were part of the contingent.

But after initial success the tide of the invasion turned. The French republicans successfully counterattacked earlier that year and had not only pushed the Spanish-Portuguese army out of France, but crossed the Ebro River and were threatening Madrid.

None of his three sons had been reported killed or captured, but he had not received news of them for two months.

Rodolfo's father was cynical of the treaty with Spain. The country was too deeply resentful of Portugal's old friendship with Britain, and in conflict could well turn sides. Together with the strengthening French army, Spain could well unleash its hostility towards either or both nations.

The present successes of the French in Spain could very likely precipitate that unwanted alliance between them, and he could picture the two countries turning on Portugal. But for now, he concluded, his sons were fighting alongside Spaniards defending Spain.

Genevieve found it difficult to keep the thread of what Rodolfo and his father were discussing. Her thoughts kept wandering, drifting back to her own recent past and all that had happened to her.

Out of respect for her they were both conversing in French, although from time to time his father would lapse into Portuguese, and she would only partly understand him. Rodolfo would then glance at her and resume talking in French, and his father would suddenly apologise to her and speak her language again too.

She could not take her eyes off Rodolfo throughout the meal. Washed, shaven and freshly dressed, he was so attractive that she found her heart pounding and a familiar heat permeating her insides. A lock of his black hair would curl out of its band and sweep over his bronzed forehead and she glanced at it thoughtfully, tempted to stroke it. Then she would gaze at his clear blue eyes. The bruise around his left eye had almost faded without trace.

For some moments she found herself reflecting on his penis, as described by Elise, and his exploits with women that she'd alluded to. She pictured him naked on top of her, her potent rescuer, saviour and lover, and smiled mischievously to herself. When Elise had said it was big, how big was big?

But immediately the word murderer filled her head. Again she pictured him killing Count de Tranville, attacking those three guards, stealing clothes from a dying man, shouting orders at her, and as the memories flashed through her mind she cast her eyes down.

And then she pondered how he had not pressed her at all for an answer to his marriage proposal. He had not mentioned it to his father, either. It seemed he had taken her desire to wait and reflect with great equanimity. Or perhaps his proposal had only be made light-heartedly, and that his intentions were actually trivial.

Having experienced so many women, and after what he'd done with Elise, was he not perhaps just playing with her; cruelly toying with her emotions as some egotistical sport? Could a man who'd done the things he had done be capable of... of loving her?

She glanced at his father from time to time, and felt instinctive warmth for him. It was clear that he loved and doted on his youngest son even though, she discovered, his wife - Rodolfo's mother - died whilst giving birth to him. Conde de Agora also admired Rodolfo; it was clear in his eyes. Yet he seemed gently critical of him in every way.

She perceived that, even though he disapproved of his other sons fighting to protect Spanish soil, he seemed to keep reproaching Rodolfo for not being with them. But it was not his manliness he was slighting. He commented that Rodolfo had been a better swordsman and horseman, and more daring than any of the other three, and chided him for his reluctance to pursue an army career at which he would undoubtedly excel.

In return Rodolfo responded by making fun of the pomp and circumstance of army life. It was a life for dunces and idle show-offs, he scoffed, making his father frown. At then his father made fun of Rodolfo's hazy plans, his boyhood dreams of being an explorer like the Portuguese navigators that went to Africa, the Azores, China, India, and the New World.

They argued over Rodolfo's old interest in Brazil and his dreams of adventure and wealth there, but Rodolfo clearly did not see what was wrong with his plans. Again Conde de Agora pointed to the urgency of what was happening at home, the conflict in which Rodolfo's patriotic and dutiful brothers were enmeshed as they spoke, and the possible fate of Portugal and its monarchy. The conflict with France was a call to arms for all European men of honour, how could he be deaf to it?

But before the argument could grow heated Conde de Agora excused himself for having hardly addressed his lovely guest, but it had been so long since he'd last seen his son.

He enquired about her family and listened with nodding grief to the tale of their deaths. It was a tale so many other French aristocrats had experienced, he explained. He still had relatives and many friends in France, all suffering in the same way.

After a few quiet moments he was prompted to suggest that she should acquaint herself with a circle of French aristocrats and friends he had in Lisbon. Luckily for them they had all escaped much earlier, and formed a circle to unite others against the revolution. They were in touch with sympathisers throughout Lisbon, as well as in Britain and Spain. They had accumulated reasonable funds and were lobbying for war, printing anti-revolutionary propaganda, seeking ways to distribute it in France and to rescue those aristocrats languishing in French prisons.

He clapped his hands suddenly. Why, his neighbour Count Jacques de Vaudville was an escaped aristocrat and a major figure among the emigres. It would be an ideal introduction to some of her compatriots. The émigré French count had a delightful wife, two daughters and a son of around Genevieve's age. They had come to Portugal the year after the Bastille was stormed in 1789, and having sold their possessions for a comfortable sum, they had arrived with enough wealth to live comfortably and buy a relatively large plot of land and a stately quinta in the hilly Sintra region - unlike some of France's destitute aristocracy.

Their uncles, aunts and cousins, on the other hand, had not been so astute, and had long since been killed.

Their quinta was a few miles away, heading sharply downhill and on the other side of numerous groves of lemon and olive trees, a wood and a river running from the hills and, eventually, finding its way to the Tagus. Rodolfo smiled at the mention of the river, for he and his brothers had waded and fished there as young boys. He wanted to show Genevieve the spot, for there was a waterfall she had to see.

She smiled at him, picturing him as a handsome boy fooling around by a river. He caught the glimmer of warmth in her eyes and returned it. Tomorrow, he suggested, they would take a picnic, there was so much to see. The area was like no other on earth.

But Genevieve declined the invitation, for she needed to be alone for a while to gather her thoughts and adjust to the magnitude of recent events and their repercussions. Rodolfo's father raised his eyebrows, somewhat perplexed. It was a beautiful spot indeed, and it would do her good to go outdoors and get some fresh air into her lungs and sun on her face. But Rodolfo's expression remained impassive, his eyes not leaving hers, probing them for an explanation. She looked down and his jaw tightened.

'In that case,' he said indignantly, 'I will head into Lisbon for the rest of the week.'

His father was surprised by the reaction and expressed his disapproval, for his son had only just returned after so long. But Rodolfo insisted that he had old friends in town he'd not seen for so long. He had catching up to do. And besides, it was June, too. There would be so much activity in town. A week was not a long time, and as he was not needed at home there was no reason for him to stay around getting bored.

Genevieve turned red, but would not change her mind. His father gazed at them both, shrugged, and excused himself from the dinner table, for he too was travelling the following day to Sintra, and he had to prepare for the journey. Many of the local aristocrats were meeting there daily to discuss the events befalling Europe, and he suggested that Rodolfo should go there too at some point.

# Chapter Ten

'Admit it, you careless little slut!' Elise hissed. 'You spilled that over me on purpose!'

There was a cackle from the bed, where pale and naked, lounging with her hands behind her head, Madame Coubette watched the scene before her with a lecherous grin.

Emelie remained silent, blinking timidly at the naked, dark-haired girl who prowled around her as she knelt on the floor of Madame Coubette's bedchamber.

Elise held two objects. 'You spilled it on purpose, didn't you?' she accused again. 'You spilled it to get my attention. You want me to punish you, then you want me to do something more to you, don't you? Answer me, you little whore. That's what you want right now, isn't it?'

'It was an accident, miss...' Emelie pleaded, but she was fibbing.

'What do you want me to do to you, though?' Elise demanded.

'I don't know what you mean, miss.'

Due to Monsieur Coubette's poor health and need for undisturbed rest, his wife had long since stopped sleeping with him, which had actually been a great relief to the sexually demanding woman. She had her own bedchamber with an enormous four-poster gilded bed, from which red drapes hung and a chaise longue stood beside. And there was a huge mirror covering almost an entire wall overlooking the bed.

Elise had been sleeping with her for ten nights, whilst Emelie was allocated a space at their feet.

That morning Emelie had brought them both a tray bearing bowls of hot chocolate, but as she handed one to Elise some of its contents spilled onto her naked breasts, and the affronted and livid girl had been right - it was not an accident.

Elise had cursed vehemently and then made Emelie lick the hot chocolate from her flesh, gloating as the maid obeyed, licking every last drop of it from the creamy slopes, even sucking some from her nipples.

Then still not fully appeased, however, Elise stared darkly at Emelie and ordered her to get down on the floor. 'Kneel on all fours!' she snapped. 'And keep your eyes closed!'

Emelie obeyed instantly, getting on her hands and knees, presenting her naked bottom. It was a beautiful bottom, she knew, and she should be punished for secretly wanting to be punished. She should be beaten for secretly wanting her bottom to be beaten.

She felt the cold, leathery surface of the phallus. It was ribbed, shaped like a large penis, and Elise rubbed it against the backs of her thighs, the insides of her thighs between her legs, up against the lips of her pussy, and after lingering at Emelie's pussy entrance, teasingly withdrew it. She then flicked the crop - the second object she held - lightly over the kneeling girl's vulnerable buttocks.

Emelie shuddered and rocked down onto her elbows, and then a spiteful snap from the crop struck her a few inches lower than the first slightly lesser swat.

'Get up on your knees again,' and she did as ordered instantly, struggling to keep her eyes closed. Something was touching her forehead. It ran downwards, over the bridge of her nose to her lips. It paused there.

'Open!'

Emelie's lips peeled apart and the phallus entered, pushing in slowly, stretching her lips even wider, her jaw immediately beginning to ache. Elise held it there, lodged halfway inside the pretty little mouth, savouring the moment, exchanging victorious smiles with the woman languishing on the bed, then eased her hips forward and pushed in a little further. 'You will take it all,' she told the girl on all fours before her, and Emelie struggled valiantly to obey. It was not just large, but heavy, and it smelled of pussy juices and leather. Elise left it lodged fully within the girl's mouth and lazily ran her fingers over her face, appreciating the feel of her closed eyelids, her cute nose, her hollowed cheeks, and her stretched lips sealed tightly around the stalk embedded between them.

'Don't open your eyes,' she warned, then something touched the insides of Emelie's thighs, switching back and forth. It was the tip of the riding-crop, skilfully stinging her legs. It slithered upward to her clitoris, tickled the lips of her pussy, then moved away again.

It came back, beneath her torso and stroked her nipples, circling them. The tip whipped her nipples softly but menacingly, alternating between them, then went away again.

Emelie's heart raced and secretly her pussy yearned for attention. Quite frankly, she admitted shamefully to herself, she wanted Elise to fuck her.

Nothing touched her for a while, their only contact being the stout leather column that bridge the tiny space between Elise's cunt and Emelie's flushed face and speared into her throat. Then she shivered, for something was tickling along her spine and tracing the contours of her buttocks. It was the riding-crop returned, but then it lifted again and she heard it being dropped to the floor.

The phallus was pulled slowly from her mouth, its ribs running off her tongue, and she sighed as her jaw was able to relax.

'Lie down.' Elise was standing and her foot was on her shoulder, pushing her to the floor, so she meekly lay flat on her front, her cheek resting on her folded forearms.

There was a tense pause. She shivered in the silence and dared to open her eyes just a little. Elise was doing something, she could just see her feet, and there was a lewd snigger of approval from the bed.

Hands lifted her midriff a little and a pillow was stuffed between her and the carpet, raising her smooth buttocks, and as she wondered what on earth was intended her feet were nudged wide apart and someone - Elise, she knew - was covering her, her soft breasts moulding to her back, her sweet breath wafting around her ear and shoulder, fingers entwining in her hair and tugging painfully while others clamped to her buttock and prised it away from its twin... And then Emelie cried out in utter shock and dismay as something large and bulbous nosed into her virgin anus, paused while she caught her breath and absorbed the enormity and shame of what was happening to her, and then sank with one inexorably slow lunge to utterly invade her tight rear passage.

Once Elise's pubic curls were nestled against the deliciously soft buttocks of the lovely girl sandwiched submissively beneath her she rested for a few moments, enjoying her triumph, and then slowly began to fuck her arse with the huge leather cock, while Madame Coubette watched the splendidly erotic performance from amongst the silk pillows on her bed.

Penetrated in such a demeaning manner, Emelie felt totally defeated, although the shameful stirrings of an orgasm were beginning, seeping from her core, filling her insides. It was uncharted but wickedly delicious territory. She sighed uncontrollably, rolling her hips to Elise's tormenting rhythm, and Elise smiled.

'This is what you wanted, isn't it?' she gloated, whispering into the vanquished girl's ear, and despite herself Emelie sighed again, lifting her buttocks higher to meet Elise's thrusts. The young mistress knew everything about her, and there was nothing she could do to resist.

For ten nights Elise and Madame Coubette had slept together and feasted on her and each other - but never anything quite like this had occurred between them...

It was after those ten days and ten nights when Elise told Emelie that she needed to take her away. They were to go on a journey. It would be safe and all she would have to do would be to act naturally and to remember to say a few certain things. She wanted her to meet her old friend Genevieve, and just perhaps, Elise could find a way for them all to be reunited and to live happily back in France...

# Chapter Eleven

After dinner Genevieve went to bed with a melancholy weariness. Her hosts were being as kind as could be, she knew, offering her their home and shelter without really knowing her or very much about her.

Her temporary sanctuary - for that was all it could every really be; her home and life was in France - was a cool and fresh one. She gazed out of her bedroom window, the stars in the night sky large and sparkling bright - even more so than in France, she was sure.

Below, in the darkness, she could just make out a strange and unworldly panorama of stony buildings, all slightly differing in gothic and Moorish blend, scattered over peaks and wooded hills.

She closed the two large shutters, then cast off her clothes and stretched out naked on the bed. She enjoyed the sensuality of the warm air on her uncovered flesh, the moonlight creeping through two cracks in the shutters, and its beam falling across the lower half of her slender, virginal body, her golden pubic hair glistening in the silvery light.

After a moment she bent her legs, raised herself onto her elbows and let her head loll back loosely. She shook her hair and felt it sweep the bed, then glanced at the closed bedroom door.

For a moment she closed her eyes and pictured Elise, smiling at her, burying her face between her legs, looking up at her capriciously as she held her artful tongue lingeringly and tantalisingly on that certain exquisite spot. And she recalled how she had in turn kissed Elise's wet lips between her smooth, fragrantly scented thighs.

She recalled how Elise had spanked her, her clitoris rubbing over her thigh. She remembered those spankings from Elise, and the beatings from Count de Tranville.

And each time it had happened. Somewhere amidst her shame, her incapacity to resist, something began awakening, and as it awakened it took control of her. And she had chased it, all the while trying to convince herself that she was at the mercy of forces beyond her control.

And then her thoughts moved to Emelie. Where was the sweet girl now? How lovely she was, but would they ever meet again?

Genevieve shrugged off the sadness thoughts of the girl threatened to enshroud her in, and remembered the night the count copulated with Elise on the dinner table, grunting, thrusting, and leering at her like an animal, and despite her abhorrence at the memory a strange and compelling tightness churned in her stomach. It was nice and she wanted more, so she lay back and slipped a hand between her parted thighs, her knowing fingers caressing the damp lips of her pussy in the peace of the moonlit room

Feeling naughty, she then lifted her fingertips to her tongue, moistened them, and began tracing circles over her eager clitoris, her pussy getting increasingly wet. She rubbed more quickly, losing herself in pleasure, placing both hands between her legs and stroking.

She felt a sigh of joy ready to burst from her but suppressed it, not wanting anyone to hear her, and then she relaxed and let herself drift, slowly falling asleep.

Genevieve awoke fairly late the next day, and by the time she got downstairs the two men had already left. She went into the breakfast room to find the table not fully cleared, and three maids stood looking out of the window, chatting idly to each other, but they span round when they heard her enter.

They were all pretty young things. Two were about her height, with olive skin and black hair tied into buns. They had a playfulness in their expressions, and she remembered being told the evening before that their names were Flavia and Fulvia.

The third girl, who she thought was called Ana, also had healthy olive skin. She was slightly shorter than Genevieve, she too had a saucy face, but her eyes were sea-green and she had light brown hair.

Her figure attracted attention too, for she had large breasts and full hips, sensually voluptuous without quite being plump. She appeared to be the most confident of them, and greeted Genevieve in broken French while the other two giggled shyly and hurriedly cleared what remained of the breakfast table.

She told them what she wanted to eat, and as soon as they left she wandered to the window, surprised to see Rodolfo outside sitting astride a horse. So he hadn't yet left for Lisbon. Instead he'd been out for a morning ride.

His horse was still sprightly so he decided to exercise it further, taking it back and forth over a white dry stone wall, the graceful beast clearing it gracefully each time. Rodolfo looked dashing, straight-backed and vigorous, and the maids no doubt had a crush on him, Genevieve realised.

He was heading for the stables and looked up, noticed her and waved. She waved back, and about ten minutes later he appeared in the breakfast room just as her food was being served.

'Good morning,' he said breezily. 'It's a fine day. How are you feeling?'

'A little more relaxed, thank you,' she told him.

'Are you sure you don't want to go to the river with me?' he continued cheerfully. 'You'd love it there, I know you would.'

Genevieve remained silent for a moment, and then gazed into his eyes. They were clear and unassuming. 'No,' she said finally, 'thank you.'

He stared at her quizzically, but she avoided his look. 'There are many things here I'd love to show you,' he told her. 'The forests are more beautiful than those in France, or anywhere else. A lot of painters and poets drift around here. We could then head west to Cabo da Roca and Collares.'

'I'd like to,' she admitted, 'but there is still much I need to think about, and I need time to do that.'

Rodolfo smiled and shrugged.

'If you care for me, as you profess to, you will understand,' she added.

'As you wish,' he acknowledged. 'But sometimes it is best not to think too much.'

She looked into his eyes again and suddenly felt he was right, and she wanted him to embrace and kiss her.

'I'm leaving, then,' he announced, still smiling good-humouredly. 'I'll be gone for a week. I hope you manage to relax and do the thinking you need. You should take walks; it is very pretty around here.'

He bade her goodbye, and it was as he turned to leave that a wave of emotions suddenly erupted in Genevieve which immediately surprised her and which she later regretted. 'Wait!' she blurted. 'Tell me, are the brothels in Lisbon as entertaining as those in Paris?'

Rodolfo turned back to her slowly, his brow furrowed. 'I'm not sure,' he said, 'I've been away for a long time. Why, do you wish to go to a brothel?'

'Perhaps, to see just how you entertain yourself whilst in Lisbon,' she said, lifting her chin defiantly.

He gazed at her silently. 'Why do you say that?' he asked.

Genevieve stared sulkily down at the table. 'As I said, I need to be on my own and I need time to think,' she said firmly, realising she had perhaps overstepped the mark, that perhaps he didn't deserve to be spoken to in such a disrespectful manner. He had, after all was said and done, rescued her on that fateful night when the revolutionaries stormed Count de Tranvilles home, and he had subsequently proposed to her.

'Please take your time doing what you feel you must do,' Rodolfo said, 'but don't spend it judging me.' With that he turned and left the room, as Genevieve did nothing but watch him go.

Genevieve's glum mood lasted through breakfast, until two of the maids came to clear it away. They smiled at her as they appeared, but when they saw the sullenness of her pretty face and the intensity of her eyes, their smiles quickly faded.

'Mademoiselle is not well?' one enquired in heavily accented French.

'I'm fine, thank you,' Genevieve replied curtly.

'Mademoiselle is still tired?' the other maid added.

'How is it that you know French so well?' Genevieve asked.

'The artist,' Ana said, for she had entered without Genevieve noticing. 'The artist is French.'

'The artist?' said Genevieve.

'Oui, the young artist is French,' Ana went on. 'He is very nice. He writes poems, and paints, and teaches us too. He is a little crazy, and all the time he wants to...'

Both the other maids looked at Ana sharply, and she instantly covered her mouth with her hands. But Genevieve was not really interested in the apparent secret that Ana had almost uncovered, for her anger was simmering again as she imagined Rodolfo making love to the three of them somewhere in the house during the night while she slept.

Genevieve had excused herself early from dinner. Having earlier returned from Sintra, Conde de Agora chatted with her politely and warmly but she was not up to the conversation. She did not care to talk about the revolution, nor did she have strong views on the current political situation in Europe.

As far as she was concerned, the revolution had swept away her family and she hated it. After that the foremost issue on her mind were her confused feelings towards Rodolfo. She struggled to return her host's pleasantries before excusing herself and complaining of a headache. He advised her to rest immediately and said he would send someone up later with a warm drink.

An early night was exactly what she wanted. She longed to undress in the warm evening air of her room again, just as she had the night before, and to ride in the moonlight on the feelings she had aroused with her own touch.

As soon as she reached her bedchamber she threw off her clothes as before, lay naked on the bed and spread her legs. She trembled in the darkness, stroking her flat tummy and pussy lips. But this time the sweet sensations did not awaken quite as readily as before.

In vain she toyed with herself impatiently, stroking with both hands, placing a cushion between her legs to angle her hips and make herself more accessible to her fingers. Eventually, with her eyes shut fast, her hands rubbing furiously over her pussy and pubis she could feel herself stirring - but then there was a knock at the door.

She exhaled heavily in frustration and scrambled under the sheets, calling for whomever it was to enter. Ana appeared with a cup of warm milk, her eyes sparkling knowingly as they met the French girl's.

Genevieve blushed red and took the cup from the girl. It was clear that she wore nothing beneath the sheets, and from the rosy heat in her cheeks and her breathlessness, the maid could draw fairly accurate conclusions about the girl's activities without too much difficulty.

Conde de Agora had breakfasted early again the next day, and once more Genevieve found herself dining alone. Her frustrations toward Rodolfo from the previous day had faded, and now she felt a mixture of loneliness and tension. Had Ana seen enough to suspect what shameful things she'd been up to? Had she gossiped about it to the others, making Genevieve an object of ridicule among the servants?

Fortunately Ana was not serving at breakfast, so Genevieve was relieved to not have to face her. Only one girl was in attendance, one she had not seen before, a fresh-faced girl with blue-black her and dark eyes. Silently and with a shy smile she served and cleared Genevieve's breakfast, and none of the others were to be seen.

Afterwards Genevieve wondered what to do. She had spent the previous day alone in the house, and so she wanted to go out for a walk. It was a bright, cloudless day and the warmth and solitude were already beginning to soothe her.

The clothes she wore were a strange mixture of items pulled together from around the house and placed in her wardrobe, and because the household had lacked a mistress for so many years, few of them were actually for a woman. So that morning Genevieve wore a tight pair of boy's breeches that must have belonged to Rodolfo or one of his brothers when they were much younger, and a white shirt that also clearly once belonged to a young man. She had to roll up the cuffs to uncover her hands.

Although unusual for a beautiful girl from good stock to wear, the outfit made her feel comfortable and strangely excited. Her hair was washed and smelled fresh, and shone lustrously that morning when she stepped out into the bright Portuguese sunshine, adding exuberance to her rosy cheeks at a time when she was feeling less than secure. She was a combination of flattering contradictions, her fresh face and appearance so feminine and so at odds with her clothes that she seemed more enigmatically alluring than ever.

Wearing a pair of cork-soled sandals she decided it was time for her to venture out and explore the verdant valley that spread before her bedroom window. So her wandering started at the old wall where Rodolfo had been exercising his horse. It seemed to be built of a different stone to the rest of the house, and looked as if it might have been far older.

From there she spotted a footpath winding downwards towards a series of groves, from where a strong fresh scent drifted upward. It was eucalyptus, an odour that was as new to her as it was enchanting, and she walked through a patch of the eucalyptus trees as if in a languid trance.

From there her senses were further filled with new smells as she wandered through lemon trees, heading downwards sharply until she reached the start of rich leafy woods.

It seemed intimidating to her at first, despite its vivid green beauty. But with little reason to yet return to the house she continued through softly shaded foliage, gradually becoming darker as she strolled deeper into the woods. Now the sunlight only flickered through crossed branches and fell in moving shafts on thick red trunks.

She stopped by one large tree for a moment, in awe of a creature she saw staring down at her. It was a tiny snakelike thing with beady, roving eyes, and as soon as she stepped closer it scurried off on four legs.

The undergrowth bristled with life. Birds seemed to twitter from every branch, and the downward descent continued with the same steepness. Occasionally she would come to a clearing from which she could still view the other hills around her, sand-coloured rocks and peaks.

After another ten minutes or so she heard the distinct murmur of water and immediately thought of the river Rodolfo had mentioned. She wanted to reach it, that would be her goal for the day, she told herself, realising that the upward return would not be as easy going as her journey so far.

But as she continued her descent the ground levelled out, and soon she came to a break in the woods and faced a wall of bushes. The water could still be heard and she wanted to press on, and was relieved when she saw that the path continued very narrowly through a break in the bushes to her right. She made her way excitedly through the gap and after a few minutes she was suddenly delighted to see the glistening light of water, flashing downwards from a rocky waterfall some four metres above ground level.

She headed towards it, still on the overgrown path, and then a sight suddenly caught her by surprise and held her in her tracks.

Not far from the water's edge there was a fallen tree, and on it sat a few figures. They had their backs to her and were observing something, chatting and giggling, and Genevieve realised they were some of Conde de Agora's maids.

She recognised Flavia and Fulvia first, sitting side by side. Next to them was the girl who had served her breakfast that morning, and beside her was a girl Genevieve recognised but whose name she didn't know.

Just in front of them Genevieve spotted another figure, a slender blonde girl standing before an easel upon which was a canvas. Although she was of slim build she had quite broad shoulders, and she wore a flowing white cotton dress. She held a brush in one hand and her face flitted intensely from the canvas to whatever scene was taking place in front of the sitting maids, out of Genevieve's view.

However, as Genevieve looked at the girl's face she gasped and her hand rose to her mouth in shock, her eyes widening, for she could not help but notice the wispy moustache and small beard on her chin. The girl was not actually a girl after all! Or if she was, she was some kind of a freak!

Despite her initial revulsion Genevieve could not suppress her curiosity, and she carefully edged closer to the surreal scene, her eyes on the freaky artist. He was about the same age as her, she guessed, not much taller, very slightly built and now noticeably effeminate, although the moustache and beard were in truth no more than sparse and wispy bristles.

His blond hair was curly and long, and his chiselled face was stern with concentration. He was quite beautiful after all, Genevieve reflected, amazed that now the initial shock had passed she could actually find him attractive instead of being utterly repelled by the sight of him.

Beside him was a folding stool, upon which he had set his paints and an open book. By now she was mere yards from the small, idyllic clearing, concealed by the thick undergrowth and stepping as lightly as possible, but still she could not see what it was the maids were observing and the artist depicting.

Engrossed by the scene before her she carefully crept another few paces forward, but a dry branch snapped underfoot. The maids looked around, and spotting her immediately they jumped up and raised the alarm. The artist stopped painting and looked too, and as they all moved the scene in front of them became visible to Genevieve for the first time.

It was Ana and two other maids. They lay naked, as still as statues, the more slender two with their limbs entwined around the busty girl in an amorous pose of seduction.

One girl held Ana around the shoulders while cupping one of her breasts, her lips by her ear as if whispering something to her. The other held Ana around the waist and dangled grapes before her mouth.

They were the last to notice Genevieve, and on doing so instantly dropped their pose and became agitated. Vexation immediately crossed the artist's face and the maids were fretting, anxious to escape the scene.

'That will be all for today, girls,' the artist said brusquely to his naked models, clearly annoyed at having his scene disturbed. 'I'm nearly done anyway, so you may dress now.'

Ana and the two other naked maids stood up, looking from Genevieve to the artist before hurriedly taking their clothes from next to the trunk upon which the other maids had sat. He took some money from his purse and distributed it to the three, but the irritation on his face soon faded, seemingly transfixed by the sight of Genevieve. She stepped to one side to let the jittery maids file past her and back up the path leading homeward.

He was looking intensely at her, so she returned his stare for a few moments before starting to turn. 'Wait,' he blurted, immediately starting towards her. 'You can't simply leave after the interruption you've caused.'

'I did not mean to interrupt anything,' Genevieve responded curtly. 'I was simply taking a walk and some fresh air.'

The artist fell silent, his eyes fixed on her, blatantly taking in her beauty without shame. She studied him in return, deciding he was vulnerable and sensitive.

'You were spying on me,' he accused her.

'I was not,' she refuted.

There was a tenseness between them, and then he laughed and approached her. 'My name is Frederique de Vaudville,' he told her, and bowed graciously.

'Genevieve de Montvert,' she replied, instinctively starting to curtsey but remembering she was wearing breeches.

'Genevieve de Montvert,' he repeated. 'The name sounds familiar. You're French... what are you doing here?'

She briefly explained her flight from her country and her stay at Conde de Agora's residence, although the mention of the man clearly made Frederique edgy.

'Please,' he said, 'I'm an artist, and often, unfortunately, there are elements of art that confuse and disturb others - nudity, for example. But at my present home there is a lack of female form and beauty. Our maids, sadly, are not appropriate for modelling, but the good Conde de Agora's maids are, and they seemed to have spare time and energy, and are keen to earn a little extra money. Conde de Agora is our neighbour, a wise and good man, but if he knew of this I fear...'

'Don't worry.' Genevieve tried to reassure him. 'It is not any of my business, so your secret arrangement is safe with me.'

His demeanour brightened instantly, and he began gazing at her intensely again. 'Would you like to take a look at my painting?' he asked. 'It isn't complete, but...'

Genevieve nodded, smiled, and approached the canvas. The three girls had been painted with such a free depiction that they looked like a very different threesome, she immediately thought. She gazed at it in silence, and Frederique studied her. She did not know what to say.

'Naturally I find the female subject extremely appealing,' he said. 'But my real interest is light and dark.'

Genevieve looked at him, a little unsure of his meaning.

'It's been a lifelong fascination of mine,' he continued. 'As a boy I would often stare at burning candles in my darkened bedroom. In my fancy I imagined a battle being waged between the light and the dark. The light was seeking to penetrate the darkness, to spread from the candle and banish the darkness and shadows from my room.'

He was looking intently at his unfinished work. 'Darkness, meanwhile, would be attacking the light back, seeking to enshroud it, to smother it, to snuff it out.'

Genevieve pondered him. Why, she wondered, was he wearing a dress?

'I've been trying to blend these ideas with females and female sexuality,' he went on, not noticing the scrutiny he was under. 'Opposites waging war, but opposites always being drawn together.'

'And the third component?' Genevieve asked, indicating Ana.

'That,' he said, 'is again a fancy. I would imagine a thin, intangible area between darkness and light, and that's what she is. It's a fertile, fragile area from which pleasure and life grow.'

Genevieve was looking at him with deep interest as he contemplated his own painting. She remained silent, and could feel her heart beating and her hands trembling; he was perversely appealing, despite his strange appearance.

'I - I should be heading back,' she said quickly, gathering her wits and turning away.

'You know...' the artist went on, 'I wept bitterly when we had to leave our home in Savoy because of the revolution. The mountains and lakes there filled me with so many wonderful dreams, and one constant dream I always had was of a... a particular girl. I never really paid attention to any other females around me. Instead I dreamed of her. I wanted to share my soul with her. I wrote poems to her, poems that only she would understand. I painted pictures which I wanted only her to see.'

Genevieve looked at the painting again.

'I've spent my life waiting for that girl,' he continued, his dulcet tones relaxing in the peaceful surroundings. 'And something tells me I've not been waiting in vain, and that my waiting may have come to an end.'

'Then you're very fortunate,' Genevieve said. 'And now I really must go.'

'Wait,' he said hastily. 'Please, take this.' He stooped and picked up the book from the low stool. It was his poetry. 'I'd be honoured if you would browse the works of my heart.'

She smiled uncertainly, but took the heavy volume.

'I'll come and collect it, one day,' he said, smiling happily, looking almost relieved. 'What an enchanting model you would make,' he added suddenly. 'All the others I've painted would look pale in comparison.' She blushed at his compliment. 'It's as if I have found the light, the light side of passion. Perhaps you might let me paint you, one day?'

Genevieve blushed. 'With, or without clothes?'

'With or without... your beauty would radiate whatever. If modesty rules you, then with, naturally. But if art is to triumph, I would prefer to depict your beauty unsheathed.'

'I really must be going,' Genevieve said, after a pause to consider the sincerity of his accolades. 'Good day to you, sir.'

He bowed theatrically and held the pose, watching her from his stooped position as she turned and headed back up the path through the bushes.


If it had been Frederique's motive to immerse Genevieve in deep ponderings and reflection, he succeeded when he gave her his book of poetry. It was certainly heavy going.

She did not just browse it, as he suggested, but instead she read each of over a hundred poems again and again over the ten days or so that followed her encounter with the artist.

They were thick with allusion and metaphor and blended his own fancies and philosophies with his ideals, and his worship of a particular girl.

The girl, however, seemed to change in each poem, and on the whole actually appeared to be two wholly different females. This, Genevieve felt, seemed to correspond in some way to what he had said about light and dark.

The maids were at first shy of her as they passed her in the house, although she was in good spirits. She realised they were afraid that she would report the incident and their activities to Conde de Agora. So, one morning at breakfast, she told Ana and the other two maids clearing the dishes that she would keep the whole affair a secret. They smiled warmly and relaxed, and from then on a complicit friendliness seemed to pervade between her and the serving girls.

Frederique visited her at Conde de Agora's house three days after they first met. It was a warm morning again, and Genevieve had decided to sit among the lemon trees. He found her there reading his poems.

As on their first encounter, he was wearing a white cotton dress. They greeted each other pleasantly and with great warmth, as if they had known each other for a long time. Soon they began discussing his poetry, and as they did Genevieve looked at him quizzically for a few moments, aware that something about him was different and then realising it was his face. His moustache and beard were gone. She eyed him curiously, thinking that if it were not for the deeper tones of his voice he was almost unrecognisable from a girl.

'But there seem to be two females, really,' Genevieve said. 'You direct your words to two girls - a good one, who is fair, and a bad one, who is dark.'

The young artist smiled and shook his blond locks. 'Yes and no,' he said. 'I do see two forms of the same girl, that complement each other to make up one. However, lightness and darkness have nothing to do with good and bad.'

Genevieve frowned ironically, but the sparkle in his eyes fascinated her.

'Light has its qualities,' he continued. 'Warmth, gentleness, softness, passivity, and the tendency to yield, for example. But it has its detriments, too; fickleness, shallowness, lack of direction, lack of commitment.'

Genevieve continued gazing into his eyes, smiling subconsciously. So strange were the thoughts and reflections that filled the mind of this young man, who looked like a girl.

'Darkness has its bad qualities. It's aggressive and destructive. It hates inactivity. It's mindless and cold. But at the same time, it never flickers from its purpose, direction or commitment.'

She continued smiling wistfully, listening intently to his words.

'I'd like to paint you now,' he said coolly. 'May I?'

She was silent for a moment, caught a little by surprise. Why would he want to paint her? 'Perhaps,' she consented. 'But tell me first, why do you dress as a girl?'

'Why do you dress as a man?' he countered immediately, and Genevieve cast her eyes down over her own clothing, forgetting she was once again wearing male cast-off shirt and breeches.

'I have no other clothes at present,' she explained. 'I have no other choice.'

'Well, I do,' the artist said. 'When I was young my sisters thought I would be very pretty as a girl, so they played games dressing me as one. Gradually I began to enjoy it, and now I feel at my happiest this way. My sisters are often jealous; they say I am prettier as a girl than they are. And it helps me when I am thinking, writing and painting.'

Genevieve gazed at him again. His sisters were right. He did indeed make a fine-looking young woman.

'Ana and the other girls,' he went on. 'They have all agreed to come and pose for me again today. I have my easel set and some spare canvases, but I've been waiting all morning. Perhaps I could make a start on my painting of you?' He held out his slender hand.

'All right,' Genevieve acquiesced, blushing despite being secretly excited and flattered by the idea. She closed the book and tucked it under her arm, and he took her other hand in his as they wandered through the groves and headed down the track through the woods.

It was pleasant but strange, Genevieve felt, instantly reminded of the times when she had first arrived at Count de Tranville's chateau, and how she would walk through the countryside with Elise. For a moment she lost herself in the bittersweet memory.

Frederique began humming to himself, smiling at her from time to time, and Genevieve felt that this effeminate young man was more familiar to her than any other person she knew or had known. His blond hair and features were like Emelie's, she reflected. His full lips were soft and inviting...

Eventually they came to the small clearing again, the easel standing as before, just beside of a small patch of soft leaves and the fallen trunk. The gently gurgling water shimmered with the flickering light of the midday sun, its ripples beating from the fall like a gentle melody.

Frederique led her to the patch of soft leaves. She gazed at it silently; it was there that Ana and the two maids had posed naked in their scene of seduction.

Without saying another word Genevieve placed the book of poetry on the little folding stool that was again faithfully beside the easel, and then slowly pulled off her shirt. The cool air by the water's edge made her breasts tingle, and her pulse quickened as the artist's eyes fell admiringly to her stiffening nipples. Then he actually reached out, very slowly, and touched one.

'How beautiful,' he whispered.

Careful not to break the gathering spell, Genevieve unfastened her breeches and eased them off her hips and down her thighs, while he watched in silence and in awe. Her smooth legs felt weak as she looked again down at the patch of soft leaves, naked before him.

'Um, how do you want me to pose?' she asked tremulously.

He took her hand. 'You're tense,' he whispered. 'Relax... lie down...' She sat gracefully on the leaves, which were cold and soft and instantly made her bottom chilly, the intoxicating moment making her feel faint. 'Lie back,' he coaxed, then picked up his book of poems and dropped to his knees beside her. 'Raise your bottom a little,' he instructed, and when she did he slipped the volume beneath her. It was warmer than the bed of leaves and she smiled her thanks for his consideration, then before she could react he closed his eyes, leant down and pressed his mouth to her moist pussy. Genevieve gasped, and with only that first tentative touch of his lips she melted in ecstasy. His tongue beat delicately over her pussy lips, bathing them in lingering strokes of adoration, and Genevieve's head lolled back, her hair sweeping the leaves and her legs falling further apart as his tongue pushed into her, exploring her soft passage. She sighed blissfully, and savoured a quiet, peaceful orgasm.

And then it was as if she was in a dream, her eyes closed for a few moments that seemed like blissful hours, and upon opening them it took her some seconds to realise where she was. There were sounds of chatter and giggles as the exquisite aftermath of her orgasm ebbed.

She looked up and immediately gasped and blushed. Four of the maids were gazing down at her, smiling, and Ana was whispering to Frederique, clearly discussing her.

'Don't worry,' he said to Genevieve, seeing her rise and the rosy flush of her cheeks. 'You were tense. It's not so easy to paint a tense model, so I did what I did...'

Genevieve scrambled up and grabbed her discarded clothes. It was as if what had just happened between them had not happened - or had meant nothing to him, had been prearranged for some deceitful, ulterior motive.

'You traitor!' she hissed, hastily grappling her clothes back on.

Frederique reached for her, as though to console her like an adult might a sulking child. 'But Gen?'

'Don't touch me!' she warned, shucking his hand away from her shoulder as she fastened her breeches and buttoned her shirt, seeing him now as a patronising, duplicitous fraud, not the sensitive and considerate young man she had naively thought him to be.

Genevieve's eyes flickered from him to the other girls. They were smiling at her - smiling at her and laughing at her... mocking her.

In a sudden panic, her mind in a whirl, Genevieve snatched up the book of poems and dashed blindly for the overgrown path heading away from the clearing. She didn't know why she grabbed the book, but she did.

Tears fell from her eyes as she ran, the bushes catching her shirt and breeches as though trying to halt her flight. In her haste to get away from the treacherous group she had left her sandals behind, but she was oblivious to the jagged stones digging into the soles of her bare feet. A storm seemed to be breaking inside her, filling her with raging feelings she did not understand but filled her with fury and sorrow.

She was furious with Frederique. With his tender nature she had bared herself to him, and he had taken advantage to do something only an intimate lover should dare do. What kind of a man dressed and behaved as a woman, anyway?

And then her thoughts jumped to Rodolfo, and the sorrow washed over her. He had proposed marriage... nobly, patiently, and she had just betrayed him with another. How could she possibly face him again, ever, let alone accept his proposal?

She wept bitterly as she ran, tears blurring her sight of the uneven path, causing her to stumble and almost fall. Was Rodolfo not a renowned fornicator, though? Was he a man worthy of being treated fairly or of having her hand in marriage?

For some reason Emelie span into her head. Why Emelie? Was it because the gentle girl was the only true and loyal friend she had ever found? If only she could see dear Emelie just one more time. Would they ever meet again?

By the time she reached the groves she had stopped running and slowed to a staggering walk, panting heavily after the strenuous run up the long, winding, and overgrown path. She was exhausted and wanted to rest, but the desire to get back to the relative sanctuary of her room was stronger.

Perhaps she should marry Rodolfo, she argued with herself.

Perhaps his philandering ways to date were just a young man's thing, as Count de Tranville had once said.

Perhaps his feelings for her were as genuine as he claimed, and he was ready to settle down into married life.

She emerged from the undergrowth and approached the rambling house, stopping to rest on the old ruined wall and catch her breath.

Curiously, there was a coach stationed at the end of the wide path that led to the large front door. Had the count returned already? Or Rodolfo, perhaps? She quickened her pace again, heading pensively towards the vehicle.

An elderly coachman with a stern dark face sat up on the driver's bench. He looked at her keenly as she approached. Someone had been to the front doors, and was heading back to the waiting coach. It was a female with blonde hair tied up into a bun, her complexion clear and fair, walking elegantly in a pale blue dress. She had a pretty countenance, and Genevieve felt her heart pounding and then soaring. She recognised the girl, even from a distance. The clothing was unfamiliar, but there was something unmistakable about the graceful figure. It was dear Emelie!

Genevieve was about to wave and shout and break into a run, but then she noticed the other figure by the front door talking to the maid, Flavia - it was the unmistakable figure of Elise!

# Chapter Twelve

Most of the voyage back to France seemed blurry in Genevieve's recollection. From the time Elise and Emelie met her at the front of Conde de Agora's home, she seemed to have been overtaken by a surreal state. It could have been exhaustion - physical or emotional - it could have been a spell of grippe.

Most of the crew on the ship were French, it seemed. She had a comfortable enough cabin, and apart from occasional strolls around the upper deck for some fresh air, she remained there through most of the voyage.

She noticed a tall, grey-haired man onboard. He was a scowling, sinister figure, and for some reason Genevieve had the distinctly unnerving impression that he and Elise knew each other, although she couldn't put her finger on why she suspected that. She never caught them together, or even exchanging passing pleasantries, but something gnawed away at her.

He was like a phantom. On deck she constantly sensed he was lurking, watching her, but when she'd turn he would not be there, the masts and rigging creaking overhead in the sea winds. She only ever caught glimpses of him, and when she looked again he'd be gone as though never there in the first place.

News of Genevieve's departure was not announced or observed speedily at Conde de Agora's home. Rodolfo did not return until the following evening, troubled and ill at ease after the festivities in Lisbon.

He had been delighted to meet his old friends and to revel with them, the street processions so vivid and colourful. But at one point, when his friends suggested they seek out the company of some girls of easy pleasure, his mood changed.

So many girls had passed through his relatively young life, he reflected. So many had brought him pleasure, and enjoyed great pleasure in return. But the betrayals were mounting too; Claudine and Juliette, who only viewed him as a way to an easy life, and then Elise, and now it seemed Genevieve had let him down too. Her rejection of his proposal of marriage was the unkindest cut of all. It had dulled his appetite for female company. And after he risked all to ensure her well-being and safety.

It was thus with a feeling of quiet dissatisfaction that he returned home - a home which seemed ghostly still as he entered. It was almost dark, with only a few candles lighting the hallway and every other subsequent room he wandered into.

Something had happened, he sensed, and his thoughts turned to his father, who he found at the dinner table, alone. Where was Genevieve? Perhaps she was unwell and resting in her room.

But a look of great sadness and deep pain seemed to be written on his father's face, gripping Rodolfo instantly. What troubled him so much?

He quickened his pace as he approached the table, feeling the urge to embrace his father, but dismissing it as a sign of unmanly weakness.

So instead he nodded to him and silently took his seat at the table.

Conde de Agora did not look up at his son, at first. There was something far too important on his mind, Rodolfo knew. He would tell him in his own good time.

As indeed he did, lifting his vacant eyes to his son after a few moments, as though only just realising he was there. His face was gaunt, and he looked older than when Rodolfo had last seen him, only a matter of days before.

'I received word regarding your brothers today,' he said simply. 'News in a letter from General Eduardo da Souza, in command of the Portuguese contingent in Spain.'

Rodolfo felt his heart sink and nausea grip his stomach.

'Your two eldest brothers, Joaquim and Joao, are dead.' The old man's eyes were shimmering with tears. He looked away from Rodolfo. 'They died bravely, some six weeks ago. They were caught in a surprise attack.'

His fork hung over his plate, idly toying with his untouched meal, now cold and unappetising.

'They were heavily outnumbered and had little chance. Most of the men fled. There was little other option. But your brothers chose to stand their ground and fight.'

Rodolfo felt himself choking inside. 'And... and Pedro?' he managed. 'Any news of Pedro?'

'Pedro is in a hospital in Spain,' his father informed him. 'He was also caught in an ambush three weeks ago. His condition is critical, the general says. All the men with him were killed. Apparently he does not have long, either. But the letter is old now, so I fear he is dead too.'

Rodolfo and his father remained silent for several minutes. Then, with a weary sigh, Conde de Agora rose from the table.

'I intend to go to Spain with some friends,' he stated. 'We are grouping tomorrow. We are old, but we can make ourselves useful.'

'But, why?'

'It is not right. It is not right for old lions to sit back and do nothing while their young cubs die.'

Rodolfo stared silently at his father for a few moments, and then, controlling the tremor that crept into his voice, he said, 'And is it any less right for young men to die needlessly in the first place, among friends that are not friends, and for causes they do not understand? And is it right for older men, some would assume wiser men, to encourage them to do so?' Rodolfo's eyes glistened too, fixed on his father's.

'I want you to stay here,' Conde de Agora continued. 'Pedro is probably dead, but I will try to find him. If anything happens to me you will be the last of us. It is up to you to look after our family home.'

He turned to leave, but with what seemed like an afterthought, he turned back to his son. 'By the way,' he said. 'Pretty young Genevieve has left you. She has returned to France. Flavia has a message from her to you. And another from the French lady who came for her.'

Rodolfo gazed quizzically at his father. 'I would not go after her,' the older man advised sagely. 'It would be far too dangerous. Besides, there are plenty of pretty girls here for you to fill your time with.'

Conde de Agora stared at his son for long, quiet moments, as though he knew he was looking at him for the very last time, and then he turned and left the room.

Rodolfo sat alone deep into the night, brooding silently.

Eventually he rose wearily and walked through the darkened house, and taking a candle from the hall, headed up the stairs, his feet moving slowly and heavily.

He paused at the doors to the bedchambers that once belonged to his brothers, entering each one in turn, glancing around each room as though hoping to see someone there.

In each room he opened the top drawer of the mahogany chest of drawers that stood there, and from each one he removed a varnished wooden box. In the last room, that of his eldest brother, he paused for a longer time, then placed the wooden boxes on the bed.

He then went straight to his eldest brother's wardrobe and removed a soft leather satchel, and sat it on the bed beside the boxes. Then, with the same methodical concentration, he opened each one and removed an ornate, silver handled pistol.

They were always fascinating for him - the three pistols given to each son by their father after they had gained their commissions in the army. He remembered how his brothers would carry them proudly in their belts as, with long-barrelled muskets, they would head off hunting. He was the only one of the four brothers never to have obtained the honourable paternal token.

His brothers had teased him playfully for not following suit and joining the army. He was the youngest, and therefore had the luxury of being more whimsical and carefree, they all considered. They admired and encouraged his talents - his cunning, agility and horsemanship, and they would listen with gentle good humour to his fanciful ambitions that were so at odds with their father's.

He opened the satchel. Inside it was a long rope with a metal hook attached to one end. Rodolfo's brother had fashioned it once, to climb into the bedroom of a young lady he had an eye on; the first and only young lady he had fallen in love with, a local nobleman's daughter. His brother had remained loyal to her, and written her romantic letters from his postings ever since.

Rodolfo slipped the guns into the satchel, and then from his topcoat he removed the dagger he had bought in France. It was his token to himself, he reflected. He had killed men with it, which was more than could be said for the pretty pistols.

His brothers and love! What a joke, and they were supposed to be so much the older and wiser than he. All three had followed the same pattern, impatiently entering manhood, then secretly pledging themselves to the eternal love of some pretty noble girl or other that they barely knew, secretly knowing that sooner or later their romantic adventures would result in little more than negotiations between their father and the girls' parents.

Had he, on the other hand, not learned the true love of women? Had he not been already learning of love from a dozen or more while he was still almost a lad and while they were making their pledges and sacrifices to the first and only ones they'd met?

Real love - was it not to be found in those lazy, solitary days... when he rode out alone, exploring fields and farmhouses?

He remembered those first women, those busty farmers' wives and coy, horny farmers' daughters, growing idle in their sun-baked yards while their men toiled in the fields and then mingled moodily to chat and drink together. That's how he had learned.

He had learned all he needed to know through those women and girls, their blushes and coy curiosity at his approach, their stares and offers of hospitality, and then their passionate submissions, the baring of themselves, their hungry bodies still fruitful and to be enjoyed, their sighs and moans, their fearful glances at doors and windows, their shuddering orgasms, the gratitude, their begging for more, for secrecy, the arrangement of trysts, and so it went on, and so many became the same from maids to noblewomen, from country to country... from week to week and year to year.

He slipped the dagger back into his pocket and laughed sadly for a moment, thinking of all three of his brothers... the soldiers!

It seemed so absurd. He could never imagine any of them killing another man. They were too nice. A sudden, intense pain shot through his chest, but he ignored it.

He remembered how at times they would squabble together, and while he would be so quick to raise his fists, his brothers would take so long to be riled, as if they believed that their differences could be solved by words, by gentlemanly dress and conduct, by simply and logically learning and obeying rules that were there for every occasion in a gentleman's life.

What an earth did they think they were doing joining a profession with no other real purpose than that of killing whosoever one is told to kill? Conduct, logic, gentlemanliness in killing for no reason and being killed for no reason?

He slung the satchel over his shoulder, left the room, and soon was heading for Lisbon.

# Chapter Thirteen

There was something different about Elise. She looked the same as ever, the same dark beauty, the same sultry grace. But something was different.

After the voyage to France they had returned by main roads to the deceased Count de Tranville's chateau. The journey was no more than three days and they stopped each night at an inn, the gentle nature of the route seemingly coordinated by Elise.

And the grey-haired man seemed to be heading for a similar destination, for much to Genevieve's anxiety, his mere presence unsettling her immensely, he rode on top beside the coachman, while the three of them travelled below.

Eventually arriving at the chateau, totally exhausted, Genevieve gratefully slept through much of two days, happy to see the back of that sinister, unspeaking man.

The chateau felt different, somehow. It was not long after the death of the owner, but already it had an air of abandonment and decay about it. Any love there had been within its walls was gone.

Only two servants remained after the count's death, the elderly cook and a partially deaf maid, and even then only because they were too old to have the inclination to move on, unlike the slightly younger members of the staff. The maid was a vacant-eyed woman who talked to herself and may well have lost half her mind as well as her hearing, so oblivious was she to the recent events that had befallen the three female residents, or even the turmoil in which the country was plunged.

On the third day, Genevieve arose feeling much refreshed and more or less herself again. She put on one of her old dresses at a little before midday, and found Elise sitting in the drawing room reading Frederique's book of poetry.

'Emelie's out walking in the garden,' she said without looking up. 'We'll be eating soon. Why don't you go and fetch her?'

Lunch was a fairly basic affair; a roast chicken, a plate of spinach and a bottle of wine, and Genevieve did not feel particularly hungry as she watched the old maid ponderously slicing the meat and serving them.

Elise sat in Count de Tranville's chair at the head of the long table, and Genevieve and Emelie sat on either side of her. She poured three glasses of wine for them as the maid left.

'To us,' she toasted, raising her glass. 'Three old friends.'

Emelie smiled and raised her glass deferentially, and Genevieve followed suit while looking thoughtfully at her dark friend. Elise's eyes seemed to smoulder, and her vitality appeared to have waned since Genevieve last sat with her at the dinner table, her fine looks somehow more those of a statue than those of the cruel heiress Genevieve remembered adoring so.

'You know,' Elise began thoughtfully, pausing to sip her wine whilst studying Genevieve over the crystal rim, 'immediately after the death of my stepfather I vowed to kill you for revenge.'

Emelie put down her unused knife and fork, looking decidedly uncomfortable.

'Oh yes,' Elise continued, 'I even reflected on how, and the ways I would slowly punish you for your interruption in our lives and in his heart.'

She finished her wine and refilled the glass. Emelie gazed from Genevieve to Elise, and back to Genevieve.

'Needless to say,' Elise continued, 'I've quickly recovered from that initial wave of fury and I no longer want to see you dead... Despite everything that has passed between us I still, deep down, care for you as a sister; believe it or not. But, regrettably, others do want to see you dead. That is why I brought you back here under their instruction, using Emelie as a lure, although now I wish I hadn't. But it is too late. I have fulfilled my task and the matter is now out of my hands...'

A chill of foreboding gripped Genevieve's spine. 'Who are these people?' she asked fearfully.

'One of them travelled with us,' Elise said. 'He was there to see I completed my assignment without wavering.'

'So, who is he?' Genevieve asked.

'He is the head of Rency's revolutionary committee, and he doesn't like you,' Elise told her. 'Assuming you loyal to the aristocrats' cause, he wants you dead, but worse; given your youthful beauty, he wants to indulge in some of his deviant pastimes with you first.'

Genevieve's eyes widened in horror and her breathing grew tight. 'But why?' she gasped. 'I've done nothing to him. I don't even know him.'

'Because,' Emelie said patiently, 'you escaped from a family sentenced to death with an enemy of the revolution, Rodolfo de Agora.'

Genevieve fell silent, numbed by what she was hearing.

'Madame Coubette is after your blood as well,' Elise continued with further alarming news.

'But why does she hate me?' Genevieve gasped.

'Because it was all part of her greater plan to marry my stepfather, until you inadvertently intervened. Once her husband died, by marrying my stepfather she would have added the capital of this estate to the huge capital her husband has already. And her plan might have succeeded, had he not set his mind on marrying you.'

Genevieve gazed at her in bewilderment, struggling to take it all in, struggling to absorb the fact that she had enemies who hated her so much they would kill her, yet she herself would not hurt a fly. 'And you wanted me dead too...?'

Elise sipped her wine again. 'For a while,' she admitted frankly. 'After all, I was jealous of you, jealous of the way he doted on you like a lovesick fawn, and angry that he was killed by your lover.'

'He was not, and still is not, my lover,' Genevieve said firmly.

'Rodolfo,' Elise hissed, apparently without hearing Genevieve's lament, 'who would take me as his whore but not as his wife!'

'I didn't mean to cause any ill feeling,' Genevieve said sadly. 'Rodolfo's actions, and your stepfather's attentions, had nothing to do with me. I did not encourage either man to behave or act as they did.'

'I know that now,' Elise said. 'That's why I no longer want any harm to come to you. But others do, and they might be coming any day now to see to it.'

Genevieve's eyes glistened with tears. She did not want to cry but she struggled to contain her fear and sadness. 'Why did you bring me back here?' she asked. 'You brought me back to a death sentence. You knew I'd die if I returned.'

'I'm sorry, I had no other choice,' Elise repeated.

The tears had begun trickling down Genevieve's cheeks, and Emelie looked at her mournfully, her eyes filling with tears too.

'I dreamed of both of you, while I was away,' Genevieve said, as bravely as she could. 'I dreamed of Emelie, and I dreamed of you, and I felt that despite your cruelty there was still something between us... there was love.'

A heavy silence draped over the three girls for some minutes, the food remaining untouched, and then Elise spoke again.

'I've been reading your book,' she said, the normality of her words seeming bizarre in the circumstances. 'It's beautiful. You know, there is so much about myself I have never really understood. And conversely, there is so much about you and Emelie I thought I did understand.'

Both Genevieve and Emelie looked at her.

'But it's as if the poet knew more about us then we do,' she went on thoughtfully. 'There's something he sees which I haven't been able to see. And reading his poems has been like a cloud clearing from my mind. I would give anything in the world to meet him... to know him.'

Elise looked at them. 'Perhaps it would have been better to remain in Portugal after all,' she reflected. 'But it's too late now. They'll be coming soon, and there's nowhere we can run to, nowhere we can hide.'

That night, and for the next few nights, Genevieve, Elise and Emelie shared Elise's large bed, finding comfort in each other's arms as they slept.

In the early hours of their third night together, a particularly warm night, Genevieve dreamt of Rodolfo, of his handsomely rugged face at the bedroom window, rising until she could see his broad shoulders too.

But then she leapt into a sitting position and clamped a hand to her mouth in shock. 'It's him!' she hissed, desperately rocking the shoulders of the girls sleeping on each side of her. 'It's Rodolfo!'

Her hushed cries startled Elise and Emelie, hauling them from their sleep, making them sit up too.

Rodolfo continued lifting himself through the partly raised window, dropping a leather satchel into the room with a heavy thud. He gazed at them for a moment. They made an appealing sight, their breasts naked, their hair dishevelled, and in the middle was Genevieve; pale, delicate, with a face as beautiful and innocent as could be.

The three girls continued staring at him as he stared at them. His black hair was tussled and clung to his sweating forehead, and dark bristles shaded his lean jaw.

He turned after a few moments and reeled up a rope that was hooked to the windowsill, winding it quickly and quietly into a ball.

'There's no need to fear,' he said, lowering to his haunches to stuff the rope into the satchel.

'You left so abruptly,' he said to Genevieve, 'and without even saying goodbye. I have some business in France, so I thought I'd stop here first to see if I could get an explanation. I think you owe one to the man who is still awaiting an answer to his proposal of marriage.'

Genevieve gazed at him. He had returned for her, and deep down, she always knew he would. 'I'm sorry,' she said, 'but you would never love only me alone, Rodolfo. So how can you say you love me? You know I love you, but...'

Rodolfo frowned. Was he in danger of making the same mistakes his brothers had made when it came to the fairer sex? He had fallen for the girl, to the point where he was seriously risking his own life for her - again.

Genevieve rose elegantly and stood before him, enshrouded in shadows. 'Trust me, Rodolfo,' she whispered. 'I understand you better than you understand yourself.'

Just then the sound of carriages approaching the chateau at pace disturbed the serenity of the scene. They drew to a halt, there was a general hubbub rising up to the open bedroom window from below, and then fists hammered on the front door, demanding entry.

'It's them,' Elise whispered, with a look of sad resignation. 'They've come for you, Genevieve.'

She rose and slipped on her nightdress. 'I'll go down alone. I might be able to change their minds.'

Elise was nervous and fearful as she left the room, a state in which neither Genevieve or Emelie had seen her before.

The front door was heard to open and instantly there were threatening demands, interspersed with the more subdued efforts of Elise to reason with the intruders.

Emelie and Genevieve looked anxiously at each other, slipping into their own nightdresses.

Elise returned, looking at them mournfully. 'They want you to come down,' she told Genevieve. 'It's Madame Coubette and the head of Rency's revolutionary committee. And he's brought his henchmen.'

Genevieve gazed at her in fear.

'It will be better if you do what they want,' Elise went on. 'They may decide upon leniency. But I don't know, they may not.

'And if they find you here,' she went on, turning to Rodolfo, 'they will kill you for sure. There are four of them, and they're all armed. There is nothing you can do. You should stay up here, or get away while you can. It is for the best. You will only make matters worse for poor Genevieve if you try something foolish.'

Genevieve looked sadly at him, nodded bravely, and left the room, Elise and Emelie following.

Madame Coubette stood at the foot of the staircase, ready to greet her.

'At last,' she gloated. 'My beautiful young countess-to-be, as delicious a morsel as I could ever wish to have in my clutches!'

The evil, grey-haired man stood behind her, a sly leer on his face. He licked his sharp teeth avariciously as he watched the three beautiful girls, and particularly the one leading, descend towards them.

Three other brutes stood close by, their hands poised over weapons.

Genevieve stepped slowly down the stairs, as if taking her last walk - which might well be the case. But she held her chin proudly high and pulled her shoulders defiantly back.

Madame Coubette held a riding-crop in her hand. It was the deceased count's. 'Now, my spoilt little slut,' she snarled. 'It is at long last my turn to do with you as I please, without any interference.' She turned slightly to her sinister associate. 'We've been waiting so very patiently for you to return here...' Her eyes narrowed threateningly. 'Now come here, you troublesome little bitch!'

As Genevieve reached the bottom step the harridan grasped her hair and twisted her downwards, so that with a squeal of agony she was forced to her knees. She buckled before the villainous gang, but they merely sniggered scornfully at the delicious sight of her cowering before them.

Immediately Madame Coubette ripped back the riding-crop and lashed it across Genevieve's unprotected bottom. She wailed pitifully, but the arm lifted again and came lashing down on the same punished spot. Genevieve fell forward on her hands, her head pulled up and back by the vicious fist entwined in her hair, tugging brutally on her roots, forcing her to look at the vile man who stood before her crying eyes as he watched the beating with evident relish. She begged for mercy, but the obsessed woman merely lashed her again, and again, and again.

The man put his hands on his hips and planted his feet firmly apart. 'You've caused us a great deal of trouble,' he eventually said. 'And you'll die for it. But on the other hand, I am a man of compassion, and I might decide to pardon you after all. It all depends on how much appreciation you would show for such a kind gesture.' He rubbed his chin in mock concentration.

'And how good a slave you'll be when I get you home,' Madame Coubette cackled.

The man gazed down upon Genevieve, on her hands and knees before him, her lovely face raised and vulnerable to his desires. Her nightdress was now a little torn, allowing him teasing glimpses of red welts striping the milky flesh of her buttocks.

Without further ado he casually unfastened his breeches, and Genevieve gasped, trying to slowly shake her head in denial of his obvious intentions. But the spiteful woman's fist held her steady.

He gripped his growing erection, rubbing it pensively as it poked from his flapping breeches, and leered at her, licking his teeth again. 'I've been waiting quite some time for this moment,' he growled. 'So now, let's see how well you suck a *real* man's cock...'

He took a step closer and Genevieve closed her eyes against the loathsome penis as its bulbous tip nudged against her lips, and she closed her ears to the vile abuse and insults being directed at her by his disgusting cohorts.

'Come on, my pretty,' he croaked. 'Don't play games with me. Don't think you can deny me. Open your pretty mouth and show me what you can do with your clever tongue and lips. Don't be shy...'

A deafening retort echoed through the hallway, like a peal of thunder. Genevieve flinched and instantly opened her eyes, and then began screaming. The evil man still leered, but his eyes were suddenly unseeing, as though he was not there. And then blood seeped down over his features, trickling around his eyes and down his nose. He staggered and tumbled, waved on his feet like a tree about to fall, and then slumped heavily to the floor with a loud thump.

Another clap of thunder resonated through the hall and one of the three henchmen was thrown backwards, hitting the closed door of the drawing room and bursting it open, disappearing out of sight as he clutched his chest, a look of shock and fear frozen on his face.

'It's him!' Madame Coubette screamed. 'On the stairs! Get him!'

The first of the remaining two henchmen lumbered towards Rodolfo, but he too lurched backwards as the third pistol shot burst forth. His body fell in a heap and Rodolfo was on the move, stepping over him with feline grace, a wild cat going for the kill. The silver handles of three pistols poked from the waist of his breeches.

The last of the three men looked terrified. All too late he seemed to realise he held a musket, but as he raised it Rodolfo struck with the speed of a snake. The man fell, instantly dead, and Rodolfo held his dagger, the lethal blade dripping red. Casually he bent to wipe it clean on the dead man's tunic, and then slipped it back into his clothing.

'You!' Madame Coubette screamed, her features twisted insanely. 'You murderous villain!' She ran at him, raising the crop again, ready to lash at him, but he caught her wrist as it swept down and pulled the weapon from her grasp. She stared at him wildly, panting, glancing at the crop in his hand. He tossed it to the floor, and she broke down inconsolably, weeping like a baby.

For a few stunned minutes there was no other noise in the hallway, other than the woman's pathetic sobbing. And then Elise spoke.

'You are no longer welcome in this house, Madame Coubette,' she said. 'It is best that you leave, and don't ever come back.'

'You won't get away with this,' the harridan snarled defiantly. 'The revolution won't let you escape. Any of you. You will all pay dearly for what you have done!'

While Rodolfo checked that the four men were indeed dead and definitely posed no further threat, Elise went to Genevieve and helped the poor girl to her feet. Emelie went to help and console Genevieve too.

'Get out of my house,' Elise said to Madame Coubette, and Rodolfo strode to the front door and wrenched it open, staring expectantly back at the defeated woman.

# Epilogue

The diaries kept by Elise and Genevieve came to an end shortly after their return to France.

I have tried to patch together what I believe may have happened to them, but ultimately the evidence is not there in their records and can only be left to speculation. As such, I have not included it within the material of this novel that is based on their writings.

The paintings of them made in Sintra leave me to assume that the quartet headed to Portugal at some point and lived together for a period. I imagine this was not long after Rodolfo killed the head of Rency's revolutionary committee.

From Rodolfo's military dress and decoration, I can only assume that he followed up on his father's wishes and joined the army briefly, perhaps in search of his father and brother, perhaps simply to fulfil the wishes of his father.

From the painting I assume he returned safely. I have no idea if the same could be said of his father or brother.

I have written to Eduardo de Agora in Switzerland again, in search of further details. Unfortunately, he is unable to provide much more.

He noted that there was once a rare book of poetry in his family's possession - an assortment of romantic and erotic poems written in French. He was sad to inform me it was not with him. It was currently in the hands of his cousin, Laurianne de Agora.

He wondered if it might have helped in some way to clarify the latter part of Genevieve and Elise's lives. I told him that it might well have done so, and suddenly began thinking of Natalie.